GROWN-UP
SUMMER

Lacie Shea Brown

ISBN: 1981462821
ISBN 13: 9781981462827

My husband, Eric, for his relentless encouragement and my daughters, Emmy and Grace—Mommy did it.

CHAPTER 1

ANTICIPATION

Lexi's legs dangled over the dock; her toes danced above the water. She smiled into the lake at her reflection. She thought back to when she wasn't allowed on the dock without a life jacket or an adult; now she was the one who supervised. The dock vibrated as her cousin ran down the wooden planks toward her. They had only been there a half hour, and already Haley had started to annoy her.

"Can you put this on me?" Haley said.

Haley handed Lexi a pink bottle of Coppertone and turned her back. The smell of coconut and summer squeezed out of the bottle and onto Lexi's hand. When she finished with Haley, Lexi rubbed the excess lotion into her already-pink knees and smiled. Since she could remember, her mom, dad, and she would pack up the car every summer and drive the five hundred miles north to spend three weeks at the family cabin on Summit Lake. Her grandparents built the cabin a few years after they'd married, and her grandma always told her that it was the best decision they'd ever made.

"Lexi! Watch! Watch me!" Haley jumped. Her head barely made it under the water before her life jacket bounced her back to the surface. "Did you see me? Watch!" her cousin screamed.

"I'm watching," Lexi lied. Her eyes were focused on the opposite shore; it was the closest people could get by car, after that they needed a boat if they wanted to reach the cabins. She wanted to know if the Roberts family boat was in the water, but the glare stopped her view just short of the boat slips.

The Roberts family owned the cabin behind her grandparents and were like a second family to her. They'd bought their cabin a few years after her grandparents, and their two sons had grown up with Lexi's dad and aunt Jeanne. Lexi couldn't make it through a summer without her aunt reminiscing about the water-ski lessons Mr. Roberts gave her when she was little.

She'd brag about a dock start, something they no longer allowed since the water level of the lake had become so low. The drought in California was affecting everything. Lexi's neighborhood was filled with brown lawns and dirty cars. She was happy to escape the routine of school and the usual drama that went along with being in junior high. She was looking forward to high school and what she hoped would be a more grown-up life.

Lexi continued to ignore her cousin and squinted hard into the sun. She could see the outline of the chalet as it rippled in the heat; it was only the beginning of June, and already the temperature was well above ninety. The sun was hot at the altitude of the lake, but with the cool water only feet from her family's cabin, it was appreciated. She loved to swim, and the heat made it impossible not to take a dip at least five times a day.

"Cannonball!" Haley's scream broke Lexi's thoughts. Water shot out of the lake and onto Lexi's legs.

"Watch it!" Lexi yelled. "You're getting my towel wet."

"Let me do it just one more time," Haley whined.

"Fine, but scoot down a little."

2

Lexi scooped up her towel and moved it and herself back away from the dock's edge. Some of her family's bags still waited on the dock for her to carry up to the cabin. It was lake protocol for everyone to help unload a boat, but since her family arrived first, no one was around to lighten the load. Her parents had taken the perishables along with their bags directly to the cabin, and Lexi was expected to follow with the sleeping bags and pillows, but she stalled. The bags could wait.

It had been a long car ride. Her parents had stopped at every fruit stand along Highway 48 and against Lexi's protests had even made a special out of the way trip to a specialty butcher shop known for its apple sausage. These, on top of stops for the bathroom, gas, and food, added an additional hour onto the already seven-hour trip.

Lexi spread her towel out; she pulled at the left corner so that it lined up perfectly with the bottom of one plank. It was the first time she'd used this towel; the bright-green and hot-pink stripes almost glowed. The terry cloth was warm when she lay down. Her thoughts drifted, and she breathed deeply at the sound of the boats hitting the dock. Occasionally, her pulse would quicken, as her daydreams would wander through moments she hoped summer would bring. When are they going to get here? she wondered.

The anticipation of arriving at the lake for Lexi was like that of Disneyland for other kids. It was something she'd looked forward to all year; she was especially excited about this one. In years past, she'd been considered a little kid, but this was the summer before she entered high school; in her mind she was officially grown up. Up until now Lexi spent her summers going back and forth between the kid and the teen groups on the lake. She never felt comfortable with either group, but like most kids, she longed to be accepted by the older ones.

Lexi had dreamed of high school since she was little. Whenever she and her friends played pretend, she'd always announce that her name was Stacy and that she was sixteen and in high school. In junior high, she'd spent countless nights imagining her life once she became a freshman at SC Valley High. She pictured cheering at football games as a member of the varsity cheer squad, driving her own car, and being the most popular girl in school with long blond hair. Lexi wasn't sure she would have any of those things, especially the long hair, since she'd just gotten her annual summer bob, but she still enjoyed thinking about them, especially the part about having a boyfriend. And the only boy she'd ever imagined as being the one was Justin Roberts.

Lexi had been in love with Justin for most of her fourteen years. He was three years older than she was. From the time they were babies, Justin and she would spend every hour of daylight together; if they weren't swimming, they were building forts or playing Uno on the deck. After sunset their families would sit around a fire, while Justin and Lexi would entertain them with campfire songs. When they were younger, their families would joke that one day they'd get married at the lake, but that had stopped once Justin went into high school. Secretly, Lexi missed the teasing; she liked the idea of her and Justin together even if it was only brought up as a joke.

Lexi lay on her back; the sun felt good on her face. They'd arrived at the lake later than planned. It was still warm, but, even with her eyes shut, she could tell it was beginning to sink below Flagpole Peak. They should be here by now, she thought. An unexpected shadow blocked the light as drops of cold water hit her face. Lexi shot up, water dripping down her neck. Haley stood above her soaking.

"Move!" Lexi said as she jumped to her feet and wiped the water, from her face. "What are you doing?"

Drips from Haley's life vest had left a trail down the dock and had started to pool where Lexi's head had been. She looked cold. "I'm done!" Haley said.

Lexi took her towel and wrapped it around Haley, who snuggled in and immediately wiped her nose on it. Lexi's eyes rolled.

"OK, you lead," she said.

"I'll beat you!" Haley promised.

"I don't doubt it."

Haley bounced up the granite rocks, while Lexi, unexcited about a race with a five-year-old, leaned down and picked up one of the four bags that needed to go up to the cabin. It'd only been two hours since her family had been there, but for Lexi it had felt like an eternity. She was sure the Roberts family was coming; her parents had talked to them last night, and they said that they'd be up today. She reminded herself it was only 5:00 p.m. and that she shouldn't freak out just yet.

She'd just returned to the dock and was throwing another bag over her shoulder when she heard it—the unmistakable sound of a familiar motor. Her heart cartwheeled; she had grown up with that sound, and without looking, she knew the Roberts family had arrived. Justin was here.

CHAPTER 2

UNMISTAKABLE SOUND

It took fifteen minutes for a boat to make it from the chalet to the cabins, but by the time Lexi had heard the familiar motor, she had less than ten minutes to slow her heart. She set the bags down and took intentionally slow steps to the end of the dock. It took everything in her to keep from sprinting. She didn't want to seem overly eager. She wished the late-afternoon wind would stop; her cherry lip balm was a magnet for her short, windblown layers. She looked down at her bathing suit; it was her first real bikini. She'd worn tankinis for years, but this year it was a bubble-gum pink and white polka-dot triangle-top bikini that tied in the back and had matching bottoms. Lexi worried she looked fat and crossed her arms.

At the store, it'd been different. Her mom had reassured her that it was a good fit and offered to buy it. Lexi accepted her offer and couldn't wait to show it off. She'd imagined herself in this very moment. Standing at the dock in her new bathing suit, waving, smiling, and looking mature as the Roberts family would pull up and Justin would step out. She'd casually offer to help with their bags, while he'd smile at her and wonder if he had a chance.

The motor grew louder. She wished she'd ignored her mom this morning when she'd suggested Lexi go without makeup for the car ride. Lexi didn't wear a lot of makeup; she'd just learned about pressed powder a month before while getting ready for the eighth-grade dance, but since then she'd gotten into a daily habit of wearing it along with mascara and lip gloss. But with the boat just a few yards from the dock, Lexi's heart sank along with her insecurities. She dropped her arms and gave a short, low wave. There was only one person on board, and it wasn't Justin. It was Mr. Roberts, Justin's grandpa.

Mr. Roberts had always been old to Lexi, and she'd never known the lake without him. Before Lexi's grandpa died, he and Mr. Roberts spent years as the hosts of Summit Lake Day, an entire Saturday dedicated to competition between cabins with the finale a big bonfire that included a BBQ and campfire songs. Summit Lake Day was the highlight of the season, and Lexi's family planned to wear team shirts this year—"Team Sterling." Anywhere but the lake and Lexi would have been mortified at the idea, but here, cheesy was appreciated.

Lexi's favorite competition was the Clothes Exchange. One person would swim ten yards to a teammate wearing an oversized T-shirt; then she'd exchange her shirt with her teammate, and the new swimmer would return to the dock. She and her friend Angela won third place two years ago, but Lexi had missed a chance to win last year when Angela's family, also longtime Summit Lakers, couldn't come. It was the first summer Lexi had spent without Angela.

Mr. Roberts cupped his hand to his mouth and shouted over the hum of the motor, "How goes it, Miss Sterling?"

"Good. Where is everyone?" Lexi tried to hide her disappointment.

Mr. Roberts cut the engine and caught the edge of the dock with his foot. He threw Lexi the rope, and she squatted to tie off the line, something it seemed she'd always known how to do. The Roberts family shared a dock with Lexi's family, which came in handy last year when they had to split the cost of repairing it.

"Well, look at you! You're practically a grown up. Has it only been a year?"

"Yeah." Lexi looked down. She didn't know if she was supposed to thank him. It wasn't exactly a compliment but more of a statement. It was also the traditional greeting from the older generation. For most families, the only chance to see each other was each summer, and anyone over the age of forty could never believe how much those under twenty had grown. It reminded her of her parents' annual Christmas party, when she'd greet people at the front door in a sweater featuring working, light-up Christmas lights wrapped around a reindeer. Her parents' friends would look her up and down and throw out the same question just as she'd offer to take their coats.

"Thanks," she said.

"How old are you now? Let's see—must be about thirteen?"

"I'll be fifteen in three months," Lexi said. "So where is everyone else?" Lexi worried she'd sounded rude and tried to make up for it by offering her hand to help Mr. Roberts out of the boat.

"Really, I swear it was just yesterday you and Justin were chasing each other. I expect they'll be here around six; just got off the phone with Nancy at the chalet, and she says they're almost past Red Oak."

Nancy was Justin's mom. She'd also grown up on the lake and had met Justin's dad when they worked at the chalet together. Nancy called the chalet with the heads-up on their arrival, because the chalet phone was the only way to reach anyone at the lake. Occasionally, if Lexi stood on the third rock, from the left side of the dock, and leaned to the right, she could get her dad's cell phone to work. Her cell never got bars. Consistent cell service wasn't an expectation. For the most part, Lexi didn't mind going without her phone. It was hard to unplug when her friends expected a response to a text or post within two minutes, but the lake gave her what her friends considered a "legitimate" reason to disconnect.

"They'll arrive just in time for tonight's BBQ. Is your grandma making her famous potato salad?" he asked.

"Yeah, I should probably go help her cut the celery; the potatoes were almost done boiling when I came down."

"All right, Lexi; we'll see you tonight. Let your family know I'm here and can help if they need anything."

"Thanks, Mr. Roberts."

Lexi picked up the bags again and followed the dock back to the granite slope that led to the cabin. She could hear her aunt, mom, and grandma laughing in the kitchen before she reached the deck. She dropped the bags in the front dorm and went into the kitchen. Lexi's grandma sat at the long wooden table her grandpa had built before Lexi was born. He was gone now, and the memorable dates and family names carved into the walnut top brought sweet memories of dinners past. She hated how her name looked. Her mom let her do it when she was nine, and Lexi blamed her for how awful it was.

"How's the water?" her grandma asked.

"Still cold."

"Well, it's early yet. Give it a few weeks; it'll warm up."

"What did Frank have to say? I saw you talking to him from the window."

"He said that the rest of the Roberts family would be here around dinnertime and that if you need anything to let him know."

She watched her grandma's hands wrestle with the potato peeler; they looked older than last year, speckled and knotted with age, but still soft. Her grandma stood up and cradled Lexi's face in her hands.

"I'm so glad you're here. Do you know how much I love you?" she asked.

"Yes, Grandma."

"Oh? No, you don't." She pinched Lexi's cheeks and rested her head against Lexi's forehead. "I love you the most," she whispered.

Lexi loved attention from her grandma; she was the family member Lexi felt closest to. Most nights, after dinner, Lexi would help her grandma clean up the kitchen, while the rest of her family sat on the deck, reliving past summers. Inside Lexi and she would gossip and giggle about the rest of them. Sometimes her grandma would laugh so hard that she'd cry. They especially enjoyed retelling the story about waking up to loud sounds coming from under the cabin, only to sneak out and discover a large, angry porcupine that sent both of them running back inside.

"Do you need any help?" Lexi asked.

"No, honey, we've got it." Lexi's mom smiled. "Why don't you go check on your cousin? I can hear her out back."

Before Lexi reached the door, she saw a flash of orange fly past the window. It'd been over an hour, and Haley still had her life vest on. She was Lexi's youngest cousin; her two older cousins were in college and rarely visited at summer. Lexi hated that she was the only one of her age in the family.

She sat on the back deck and watched her cousin play horseshoes with Lexi's dad, her uncle JR, and a few others from the upper cabins. The trail leading to the Roberts family cabin cut across the horseshoe pit, and Mr. Roberts just missed getting hit by a determined, but nowhere near the target, attempt by Haley.

"Whoa! You have to appreciate her enthusiasm." He laughed as he dodged out of the way.

Haley blushed and hid behind her dad before being reminded to apologize.

"Oh, don't worry about it, sweetheart. I need to be reminded to watch my step, especially up here. One bad foot placement and you're out of luck. I should head down to the chalet and wait for everyone," he said.

"Tell them I'm excited to see them," Lexi said. Then she quickly looked around to see if anyone seemed interested in her not-so-subtle enthusiasm.

About forty-five minutes later, before the sun slipped off Flagpole Peak and turned the lake gray, Lexi heard it.

CHAPTER 3

ARRIVAL

"Lexi!"

She strained her eyes to see past the fading light into the boat. All the memorable voices were there, but the only one she really listened for was Justin's.

"Hey, Lexi!" It was him. Justin had finally made it to the lake. The anticipation of his arrival crashed into the excitement of him being there, and Lexi's heart pinballed against the hundreds of butterflies that had taken flight at the sound of his voice.

The boat was still feet from the dock but close enough for her to count an extra person. Mr. Roberts and Justin's dad, mom and little sister, Ellie, were there; even Buck, the Robertses' thirteen-year-old black lab, was there. But she didn't know who the girl next to Justin was.

"Is that you, Rick?" Her dad's yell interrupted Lexi's confusion. He had come out of the cabin to help unload the boat and brushed past Lexi to catch the line and pull the Robertses' boat into the dock.

"Hey, Brian! Long time no see!" Justin's dad grabbed Lexi's dad and pulled him in for a hug. Lexi's entire family came to help. Lexi politely pushed through the group to reach Justin at the end of the dock. He was wearing his USC baseball hat. Lexi remembered the first summer he'd worn it. He told her he hoped to attend USC on a water-polo scholarship. She remembered because she'd felt special that he'd told her; it'd felt like a secret.

Justin reached out and squeezed Lexi around the shoulders in what felt like an obligatory hug.

"I want you to meet someone." He smiled. "This is Natalie, my girlfriend."

"Oh! Hi!" Lexi was awkwardly enthusiastic. In all the years she'd known Justin, he had never once talked about girls, and this summer she'd hoped she'd be the one to change that. Instead, she stood in front of a slim, pretty brunette with dimples and a smile that made Lexi question everything about herself. Lexi was pretty too; she wasn't as thin as Natalie, but she wasn't much bigger. Lexi had blond hair and blue eyes and was shorter than most everyone. If someone tried to describe her, the word "cute" was used in abundance. Cute and innocent, two words she couldn't seem to shake.

"Justin told me all about you on the drive up here. It's nice to meet you," Natalie said as she hugged Lexi tight around the neck. Natalie let go before Lexi's arms could react out of reflex and hug her back.

Lexi glanced over her shoulder. "Nice to meet you too." She wanted out, but the dock overflowed with multiple generations of Roberts and Sterlings. A quick escape didn't seem likely; she was finding it hard enough to stay out of Justin's and Natalie's personal space.

Justin's mom popped her head over Lexi's shoulder. "Hi, Lexi. How are you, honey?" Lexi loved Nancy and turned to meet her with a hug. She didn't want to turn back to face Justin. "This is Natalie's first time at a lake. You'll have to help Justin show her the ropes."

"Definitely." Lexi stumbled forward as Justin unknowingly bumped her from behind with a sleeping bag. "Sounds good," she lied. "Here let me take those for you." Lexi reached for two of the three grocery bags Nancy was holding and used the chaos of welcome hugs and offers of help as a chance to escape. She made it to the Robertses' cabin first and set the bags on their front deck just outside the cabin door. The dark purples and oranges of the late sunset had finished their show; it was dark now, and Lexi used the loss of light to slip back onto her deck unnoticed.

She tried to swallow the knot in her throat, but it was too tight. She fought with everything she had, but her eyes filled too fast and burned too hot for her to stop the tears. Instead she tried to slow her breathing and used the sleeve of her oversized, faded Summit Lake sweatshirt to wipe her eyes. Maybe if she allowed herself a moment of self-pity she could pull herself together in time for the BBQ.

An hour later, she sat in a deck chair tucked inside the shadow that the light from the Roberts family cabin cast, her knees pulled in tight to her chest. The laughter from inside overflowed onto the deck as more people pushed into the cabin.

Occasionally, she heard Justin's laugh. Lexi had told her mom that she wasn't hungry when she'd come looking for her, which was true. But it wasn't because she felt full; it was because she felt empty. She hadn't pulled herself together; she'd only fallen apart more. She hated how easy it was for her to cry; it embarrassed her and made her feel like a little kid.

Lexi had already slipped into the loft by the time her family came home. The creak of the deck and loud whispered reminders to be quiet made her feel safe, and she felt her body give in to the exhaustion of hurt. Her head relaxed heavy on the pillow, while her swollen eyes followed random beams of light across the ceiling. She heard her aunt remind Haley not to point the flashlight in anyone's eyes. Everyone was home; she could sleep.

She wasn't sure how long she slept, if it'd been a few hours or only minutes. The loft held the afternoon heat and made it hard to get comfortable. Lexi unzipped her sleeping bag and stared at the ceiling. A thin strip of light between two beams held her concentration briefly, before thoughts of last summer crept in. It was the first time her mom had allowed her to drive into town with Justin. She remembered every second of the trip from the time Justin helped her climb into his grandpa's truck to the cost of the groceries. It was the first time Lexi had felt grown up. But now, in the quiet of the dark, she felt small, and her newly released tears felt like proof.

CHAPTER 4

BORROWED

The smell of coffee woke Lexi, and she climbed down into the kitchen.

"Good morning, honey; feeling better?"

Lexi was relieved; her grandma was the only one awake. She sat in one of the four rocking chairs her uncle had bought while on a surfing trip in Mexico. Her grandma patted her lap. "Come here."

For a moment Lexi hesitated; she felt too big for her grandma's lap. But memories of its comfort pulled her in, and she found a way to sit without sitting. Her grandma scooped Lexi's hair off her neck and delicately twisted it into a bun. "I used to wear my hair like this all the time when I was your age." Her grandma's touch soothed Lexi, and for a moment, she forgot about Justin. "How about I make you some hot chocolate?" she offered.

"Sounds good," Lexi said.

Lexi took her mug onto the deck. The lake was still and beautiful. A few minutes later she heard the door to the Robertses' cabin open and looked to see who it was. Justin caught the door before it made the familiar slam. It was easy to tell he hadn't been awake long. His light-brown hair stood up in patches, and his right hand rubbed his eyes before he put on his sunglasses. The cool morning air hung heavy dreading the heat to come.

Lexi stared at him, willing his head to turn, but the hope of catching him alone fell. Justin turned to hold the door as Natalie, her hands full with coffee mugs, used her hip to push through. Lexi watched their brief exchange of smiles, before their arms wrapped around each other, and they turned to the view.

"Lexi!" Haley crashed out of the cabin, her voice as loud as her yellow bathing suit and tutu, and grabbed for the back of Lexi's chair. "Can you take me to the point?"

"Haley! Where are your shoes? You need shoes; you're going to get splinters." Haley's arms held her bare feet briefly above the deck, before they relaxed and dropped her back behind Lexi only to do it again. "Go get your shoes." Lexi stood to follow Haley into the cabin.

"Hey, kiddo." Lexi caught Justin out of the corner of her eye, before she turned to face him and Natalie. The word "kiddo" stung her ears. She hoped for a moment that Justin was talking to Haley, but she was already inside twirling around the coffee table singing a rough, incorrectly worded version of "Shake It Off."

"Where were you last night? You missed the singing," he asked.

Lexi returned Justin's one-dimpled smile, before her insides flipped and her glance fell to the ground in search of composure. Be normal, she told herself.

"I didn't feel good."

"Are you feeling better?" Natalie asked. Her words made the voice inside Lexi's head scream "oh my God" louder than it already was. Lexi couldn't believe how much this sucked.

"Yes." Her words came slow, but her thoughts raced. "Thanks." Lexi tried to remind herself that she was friends with Justin. This conversation shouldn't be awkward. How could she make things less awkward? Small talk seemed appropriate. "So how'd you guys meet?"

"School," Justin said. "We were in the same English class last year."

"Oh, cool. How old are you?" Lexi only heard how oddly timed the question sounded after asking it.

"I'll be eighteen in two months. God, that sounds so old." Natalie turned into Justin with a giggle. This was awful. Lexi's lips pressed together, and she took a deep breath through her nose. She didn't want to watch them flirt.

"Not that old." Lexi attempted a smile. She wanted Justin's attention, and she desperately hoped he was oblivious to her discomfort. This was so far removed from the summer she'd envisioned. Her daydreams of flirty conversations, the possibility of handholding, and the desperate desire for a first kiss were so loud inside her head.

"What grade are you in?" Natalie asked.

"I'm going to be a freshman." It was such a weird feeling. In another time, another place, anywhere besides the lake, Lexi could have handled this, but this was her lake. This was their lake. It didn't matter that Natalie was nice; she didn't want Natalie to matter. Natalie wasn't supposed to be here. Justin wasn't supposed to have a girlfriend.

"You're going to have soooo much fun in high school," Natalie said.

"Yeah. I'm excited." Lexi's smile wasn't coming as easily. Questions, doubts, and frustrations; Lexi's brain was dizzy with whys. "What are you guys doing today?" Her eye contact with Justin was sporadic. If she could just keep the conversation casual, things would be OK.

"I thought we'd kayak to the old Boy Scout camp. Can we borrow yours?"

"Sure." What was happening? Was this seriously happening? Why? Lexi wanted to die. Was Justin really asking to borrow her kayak to take Natalie out? The conflict between wanting to scream and to keep breathing pulled the knots in her stomach tighter. She convinced herself to breath.

"Thanks. We'll probably be gone for a couple of hours. We might get out and hike a little, before we come back. Is that cool?"

"Cool. Sounds good." See? Lexi told herself. I'm totally OK with this. She and Justin were friends; it didn't matter that he had a girlfriend. Her friend was asking to borrow her kayak; it was that simple.

Natalie and Justin headed toward the water, and Justin gave a quick wave over his shoulder. Lexi couldn't help her smile as she watched Natalie follow Justin in an awkward sidestep down the granite slope to the lake. There wasn't a defined path, but Lexi could walk that slope in her sleep. She'd crisscrossed the distance from her cabin to the lake thousands of times in her fourteen years. In one day, she might go from her deck to the lake as many as thirty times.

Natalie and Justin's conversation couldn't reach Lexi from the dock. She watched as Justin sank easily into his red kayak. The patch he'd put on two summers ago still held. He and Lexi had been in the channel between the upper and lower lakes when he hit a rock in an attempt to splash Lexi. He jokingly blamed her for the hairline crack and swore that had she not used her paddle to push his kayak, he would have soaked her and avoided the rock.

A small but loud yelp escaped Natalie as she fell into Lexi's kayak. The surprise yell sent a flock of geese that'd gathered at the point into the water. Lexi's thoughts painstakingly backtracked through the conversation she'd just had. Had Justin really just called her "kiddo"?

"I got my shoes on! Can we go now? Please!" Haley begged.

Lexi released the breath she'd been holding and shook her head as she looked up at the sky. "We can go. I'll get your towel. Come on."

Lexi saw Natalie and Justin push away from the dock, and immediately he used his paddle to splash her.

CHAPTER 5

BFF

There were two parts to Summit Lake—an upper lake and a lower lake. The point jetted from the bottom of the channel that ran between the two. It was a popular spot to sunbath and swim because the granite shore sank smoothly into the lake, creating a shallow, level wading pool. It was a good place for Haley to play; the water was warm, and there were plenty of rocks to throw. Lexi reminded Haley to keep clear of the fire pit; it'd be a surprise if she stepped on a nail since it'd been three years since fires were allowed, but Lexi didn't want to risk it.

When Lexi was little, she and Justin were sometimes allowed to sit on the shore at the bonfire with the older kids, before her mom or Justin's would walk down with a flashlight and remind them it was bedtime. She hated when she saw the light of the flashlight, but knowing Justin had to leave too helped ease the disappointment.

She remembered the first time Justin got to stay later than she did; she was eight, and Justin was eleven. She saw her mom coming with the flashlight, and she elbowed Justin. He looked up but didn't seem fazed. He told Lexi he was going to stay, that he'd asked his parents, and that they thought he was old enough. Lexi's mom reached the group and signaled for Lexi to follow with a nod of her head toward the cabin. Up until then, it'd been rare that Lexi had noticed their age difference, but from then on, it was hard to ignore. Lexi was especially crushed when Justin got to climb Flagpole before her.

Flagpole sat a half mile across the lake from Lexi's cabin. Two trails led to the top. One was supposedly easier, but Lexi had only attempted it once with Justin and two others, and she was certain they'd taken the difficult route. From her family's deck, she could barely see the pole at the top, and depending on the age of the most recent hikers, she could use binoculars to see a bra, boxers, or a flag flapping in the wind. Lexi's parents made her wait until she was twelve before giving her permission to climb it, and even then a thunderstorm kept her from reaching the top.

"Lexi, come in with me," Haley begged. "You said you'd go swimming."

"No, I didn't," Lexi reminded her. "I said, 'I'd take you to the point.' I didn't say anything about swimming."

"Please?" Haley whined.

Lexi understood Haley's frustration and disappointment. She knew what it was like to be the only one her age and not have someone in the family to play with, but her mind was so filled with Justin that the strength of her empathy was weak. "Not right now. Maybe later. OK?"

Lexi wanted time to think. She could stand there while Haley played, but that was as much interaction as she was capable of. She was focused on Justin. She wondered how long Natalie would stay. Lexi could handle a few days with her, if it meant she'd eventually have Justin to herself. Even if nothing happened, time alone with him meant everything. Because time alone with Justin allowed for possibilities, and all those possibilities gave Lexi butterflies.

Lexi sat back on her hands with outstretched legs; she watched her toes to see if the waves created by the occasional motorboat would ripple over them or fall short. The granite was already collecting heat, and the cool water that reached her feet felt good. Lost in her thoughts of Justin and what might happen, she didn't see the canoe until she heard a familiar yell. "Lexi!"

"Angela! Oh my God! It's been forever!" Lexi felt a weight lift.

Angela's family had a cabin across the lake, and she and Lexi spent many days paddling between the two. Lexi saw Angela every year in her family's annual Christmas card, but it'd been two years since they'd hung out. Angela's older brother, Garrett, was good friends with Justin, and when they were younger, the four of them played together.

"I know! How are you?" Angela stepped out of her canoe into the water and let it float close behind her. "It's been at least one summer. Is that Haley? She's so big!"

"I know, right?" Haley was oblivious to Angela; she was busy collecting rocks. "Definitely one summer, because that's when we won third place in the Clothes Exchange." If there was one person at the lake who could help Lexi with Justin, it was Angela. "Remember, I was going into seventh grade, and you were going into eighth, and Garrett was going to be a freshman."

"That's right." Angela laughed. "I totally forgot about that. Wait! That was also the summer you told me you were in love with Justin. And remember, you got mad at me because I said I liked him too?"

"Oh God, that's right!"

"Hey, I saw him yesterday at the chalet when he got here. Did you know the Millers are letting me and Garrett work there? Cool, right? Anyway, I got to meet his girlfriend. What's her name? Nicole? She seemed nice."

"Her name's Natalie. She's actually in my kayak right now."

"What? How'd that happen?" Lexi wondered the same thing but knew she didn't have much choice. The Robertses were like family, and it was normal to borrow boats. She'd taken their sunfish sailing last summer, before her family's sailboat had been removed from under the cabin after storing it for winter. Justin asked to be polite, but the reality was there was no way Lexi could have said no.

"Justin wanted to take her to the Scout camp, so I said he could borrow it."

"Well, that was nice of you."

"What else could I have said?" Lexi wondered.

"I don't know. Maybe something like, 'You can't borrow it because I'm in love with you, and I can't stand the idea of you going anywhere on this lake with anyone but me.'"

"You think that would have worked?"

"It might have made him think twice," Angela suggested.

"Maybe." Lexi laughed. "Hey, do you remember when the four of us tried to hike to the top of Flagpole and that thunderstorm hit?"

"I totally thought we were going to die," Angela remembered.

"I was so scared. If I hadn't forced myself to move, I'd still be on the side of the mountain."

"Even the guys were scared. Remember how Garrett started yelling? And then Justin kept reminding us that he'd done junior lifeguards earlier that summer and that he was completely prepared for any emergency. Whoa!" Angela dodged to the right.

"Haley!" The rock Haley had thrown would have hit Angela had she not moved. Instead, it hit the inside of her canoe with a loud bang.

"I want to go back to the cabin," Haley demanded.

"All right, how about you try asking me instead of throwing rocks? Can you tell Angela you're sorry?"

"Sorry."

Lexi took Haley's hand and pulled her around to face her. As she started to unbuckle Haley's life vest, she looked back at Angela. "How long are you up for?"

"Garrett and I are here for the summer. School doesn't start until September, and since the Millers are letting us work at the chalet, my parents said it was OK if we wanted to stay up here with our grandma. My mom and dad will come up here some weekends, just not full time."

"Awesome. So the Clothes Exchange? Maybe we try for first place this year?" Lexi suggested.

"Definitely!"

CHAPTER 6

JUST MAYBE

Lexi and Angela said their good-byes, and Lexi pushed Angela's canoe out into the lake. From where she stood, she could almost see the top of the channel. She knew it'd be hours before Justin returned, but she stretched her neck, on the off chance she could catch a glimpse of him.

"Can we go now? Please!" Haley was anxious. The laughter and yells of hello were loud. More families had arrived overnight, and the decks were crowded with people hugging, large coolers, and barking dogs. This is what Lexi loved most. The families in the five cabins closest to hers were like family, and because the lake was so far removed from daily schedules, traffic, and deadlines, it didn't matter how much time or distance separated them. When they were at the lake, the lake was home.

"Yes, we can—" A shriek interrupted Lexi. The splash was loud. Lexi guessed it was a cannonball. And without seeing who it was, she had a pretty good guess that is was Bean. Bean was the first to jump off the dock every morning. "Yes, we can go. Let's see what everyone is up to." Haley was already ten feet ahead of her. "Be careful!" It was obvious Haley was repeatedly stepping on sharp pebbles. Lexi shook her head; she never went anywhere on the lake without her flip-flops.

"I see Aly!" Haley moved into an awkward, painful skip. Aly was Bean's daughter, and she was adorable. Lexi never saw her in anything other than pigtails. Aly's arrival meant almost as much to Lexi as it did to Haley. Aly and Haley were the younger version of Lexi and Angela. Having Aly at the lake would take some of the babysitting responsibility off Lexi.

"Can I go play at Aly's?"

"Let me walk you over. I want to make sure Bean is OK with it."

Bean and her husband were lucky enough to live within an hour drive of Summit. Unlike the majority of the cabin owners, they visited their cabin year round. Lexi hadn't known Bean's real name until last year when she heard Bean's husband call her Cindy. But even then, Bean had always been Bean, and Lexi wasn't about to switch to Cindy.

"Hey guys!" Bean was loud and jovial. Her energy was contagious, and Lexi enjoyed watching her. She told it like it was and was happy to help with whatever was needed. "I saw your dad and mom this morning. Did your grandma make it up?"

Haley and Aly were already inside Bean's cabin, a box of Barbies had erupted onto the floor. Lexi knew those Barbies well. She and Angela had played with them when they were little. The box floated between the cabins landing wherever they were most desired. It'd been a long time since she'd seen the box.

"She did. We missed you guys last night. I was hoping to get one of your famous cookies." Bean was known for her cookies; she refused to give out the recipe, but rumor had it cornflakes were one of the secret ingredients. Surprisingly, they didn't have chocolate chips, which were usually a must if Lexi was going to eat a cookie, but for whatever reason, maybe the cornflakes, Lexi was a fan. Caught up in conversation, she'd forgotten about last night until now. She wouldn't have wanted a cookie, Bean's or not; she'd felt too sick over Justin.

"We had to wait until Tom got done with work. We were up here last weekend. We're hoping to have a week this time. Aly is so excited to compete in Summit Lake Day. She thinks she's got an advantage because she's up here so often."

"I don't doubt it. Hey, do you mind if Haley plays here for a while? You can send her back our direction anytime."

"Of course. It's easier when Haley's here anyway. She keeps Aly busy," Bean said.

"Thank you." Lexi walked back toward her cabin. She looked at her watch; a little over an hour had passed since she'd watched Justin and Natalie disappear into the channel. She was torn; she wanted them to be back, because she hated not knowing what Justin was up to, but she also had zero interest in watching Justin and Natalie together. She couldn't stand the way Natalie looked at him. She knew the reasons Natalie liked Justin, but she hadn't figured out why Justin was interested in Natalie.

This was supposed to be their summer. For so long Justin had seemed out of reach, but this summer put them both in high school. And it wasn't crazy to imagine a senior dating a freshman. After all, Lexi's dad was four years older than her mom; Justin and she were only three years apart. And while Lexi had little hope for a long-term relationship with him, she did have incredibly high hopes for a summer filled with moments that would keep her heart somersaulting into next summer. The arrival of Natalie had done more than just mess with her daydreams; in fact it'd prevented her from imagining anything other than what Justin might be doing with Natalie.

She ducked inside her cabin and found a seat on the couch. Sick to her stomach, she worked to curl onto her side. Her sunscreen-soaked skin plus the heat made the faux leather sticky. She hated this couch. Besides being incredibly uncomfortable, the cushions slid off with the slightest movement. Within an hour, she was laying on the springs between the back of the couch and the cushions that had slipped forward just enough to make room for her. In her mind, she'd just settled on some sort of Velcro as the solution when her dad walked in.

"I hate this couch." Lexi sat up and resituated herself. "The cushions never stay on."

"I know it's not the most comfortable thing, but it's so hard to get things up and down the lake. I think we're stuck with it, at least for this summer. We can talk about replacing it after we close the cabin for winter."

"You always say that. We've had this couch for eight years," Lexi reminded him.

"You're right. It's just hard to get everyone to agree on something. Maybe this will be the year. Maybe you can take it on as a project. Find a few styles, price things out. I really think it's a matter of someone taking the lead."

Lexi laid back down. "Sure, Dad."

"Well, think about it. So did I see Justin and his girlfriend take your kayak this morning?"

Lexi couldn't get away from it. "Yeah, they went to the Scout camp."

"Well, since you can't go for a paddle, want to go sailing with me?"

Lexi used to sail with her dad a lot, but the older she got, the harder it was to sit comfortably on the boat. The sunfish was better suited for one, especially if you planned on going anywhere. The weight of two people dragged the boat down and left little room for quick maneuvers.

"No thanks."

"You're sure?"

Lexi nodded.

"OK," he said. "I'm off."

Lexi closed her eyes. She felt half-guilty for saying no. She knew her dad missed doing things with her. They used to do a lot together, but this last year Lexi had found more time for friends and less for her dad. The lake was a good reason to spend time with her dad, but she didn't have it in her today. Today, she would lay on the couch, maybe sit on the dock and, in an effort to feel better about saying no to sailing, probably play a round of horseshoes with her dad and uncle.

"Hi, Justin." Lexi heard her dad on the deck. "It's Natalie, right? Did you enjoy your paddle?" he asked.

Lexi sat up. Her dad had run into Justin and Natalie before he'd made it to the sailboat. She waited for Natalie's answer; she hoped for the rare chance that Natalie hated it and wanted nothing more than to escape the lake.

"It was nice. A few too many mosquitoes at the camp, but it was very pretty."

Lexi rolled her eyes. Of course there were mosquitoes. If Lexi was honest, she hated them too, but she needed to come up with reasons why Natalie was bad for Justin. Complaints about the obvious seemed a good enough one. She shut her eyes hoping Natalie would provide another.

"Is Lexi around?" Justin asked.

"She's right inside," her dad said. "Lexi? Justin is here."

Justin's head popped inside the door of the cabin. The outline of his familiar frame against the sun pouring through the door left Lexi feeling self-conscious. He could see her, but his face was in shadow. He stepped inside, and she relaxed at the sight of his smile. She couldn't help it that Justin made her feel good. Natalie or not, if she was near Justin, she was happy.

"Thank you for letting Natalie borrow your boat. I think you'd be impressed by how well she did, considering it was a first for her."

"Happy to help." She was sure her cheeks were flushed. For the first time since he'd arrived, Lexi was alone with him. She was vaguely aware that her dad and Natalie continued to talk out-side. Her hands went to her hair and repeatedly twisted it into a failed bun. Giving in, she let her hair fall and tucked it behind her left ear. "But I'm sure I could still take her in competition." She laughed. It was that easy. A moment alone with Justin and she re-laxed into her confidence. She still felt nervous, but it was the good kind; more importantly, she felt like herself, and she liked herself.

"Maybe." Justin winked.

Lexi saw her opportunity. "So am I going to get the chance? Is Natalie going to be here for Summit Lake Day?" Lexi held her breath.

"It depends. She plays soccer, and if the team they played against last week loses on Thursday, she'll have to go back Friday for the playoffs."

"Oh!" Lexi realized her response sounded more hopeful than disappointed. She tried to recover. "So, in a way, it's better if Natalie can't stay." And before she'd completely given herself away, she said, "I mean." She took a breath. "It means her team gets a spot in the playoffs. Right? That's good."

Justin didn't flinch. "I guess you could look at it that way..." There was that smile again. But it wasn't just his smile. It was his smile, the eye contact, and, most butterfly inducing, a pause. He saw something—something about her, something about Lexi made him lose his train of thought. "Then again," he continued, "maybe you're just scared to lose." The pause was just long enough for Lexi's stomach to clinch. She felt something, and she couldn't help but wonder if he felt something too.

CHAPTER 7

FROZEN IN TIME

"Hey, guys." Natalie stepped into the cabin. She reached for Justin's shoulder and hung her arm from it. Justin looked at it briefly and then back at Lexi. Lexi watched Natalie take in her surroundings. Decades of Summit Lake Day awards dangled from the ceiling. They were grouped together by year, each collection uniquely designed by the family that'd volunteered to make that year's awards. There were the recently framed old advertising posters that promised the best skiing and après-ski hot chocolate on the mountain above the couch and oars that went to canoes long retired were wedged in the overhead beams. Most prominent was a stone fireplace that took up much of the floor space.

"Wow…this is incredible." Natalie seemed genuinely impressed. "Are all these from Summit Lake Day?"

Most cabins were built in the 1930s and had a room with a fireplace, a kitchen, and, if you were lucky, a connected bathroom. Their size provided enough room for only the necessities. Thankfully, the Sterling cabin was an exception. Lexi's grandpa had added two sleeping dorms on to the cabin in the 1970s. The dorms were a luxury, as most other families spent the night in the same room or on the deck in a hammock.

"Lexi and I were just talking about Summit Lake Day. She thinks she can beat you in the kayak competition."

"Well..." Natalie's eyes scanned the ceiling once more and then fell on a collection of hand-painted wooden plaques decorated with mermaids, sailboats, or sunglasses depending on the year. "Are these awards too? So cool. Well...she's probably right."

Lexi saw an opportunity to dodge Justin's accusation. "No, we were actually talking about your soccer team. Justin said you might make the playoffs?"

"I'm not sure. It's kind of a long shot, but there's always the chance. The team that needs to lose is really good. Actually, I wouldn't be that disappointed. I've been looking forward to Summit Lake Day since Justin first invited me. Maybe you will get that chance to beat me."

Natalie dropped her arm from Justin's shoulder and walked closer to the plaques. "Is this you?" Just above the plaques rested a corkboard, heaving with old chalet receipts, reminders for toilet paper, spare keys, and a multitude of pictures. Natalie pointed to a picture of Lexi, Angela, Garrett, and Justin playing Uno in the loft. If Lexi had to guess, she'd say she was about seven in that one. She loved that picture; it was a rare shot. So often the four of them were left on their own to explore and play that there was rarely an adult around to take a picture of them. Another photo was of Justin and Lexi huddled together at last year's bonfire.

Justin walked to the corkboard for a closer look. He smiled at the memory. "That's me. We spent hours in the loft when we were little; I think I was nine?" Then he reached for the picture from last year and unpinned it. "Hey, you were supposed to give me a copy of this one. It's one of my favorites." He looked from the picture to Lexi, his eyebrows raised, waiting for an explanation. He was right; she'd meant to give him one, but instead she'd kept it for herself, framed it, and sat it on her nightstand at home. It was one of her favorites too. "Do you think anyone would mind if I took this?"

"No, go ahead," she said. Standing in her cabin, watching Justin pocket a picture of the two of them, Lexi no longer felt intimidated by Natalie. In her mind, if anyone should feel uncomfortable, it was Natalie. Lexi had fourteen summers worth of lobster-red sunburns, campfire sing-alongs, sunrise fishing, bonfires, hikes, s'mores, heated family board games, tipped canoes, ghost stories, and more than twenty Summit Lake Day awards dangling from the ceiling. She also had countless days and nights with Justin. The night of the bonfire picture, she was three months from turning fourteen, and she'd hoped that would be the night of her first kiss.

It was Labor Day weekend, which meant the end of summer at Summit. Angela and Garrett were busy helping their family close their cabin for winter, and most of the other kids on the lake had already taken off for the season. But Lexi and Justin's families had plans to stay until midweek, which meant they'd had the day to themselves. Lexi hadn't had a day alone with Justin in years. Since Justin and Garrett had started high school, they'd pulled away from her and Angela spending more time with the other high-school kids. They stayed up later, occasionally snuck beers from the coolers, and played truth or dare at the point. Lexi wasn't interested in a beer, but she was jealous that she couldn't stay up as late or hangout at the point past 9:00 p.m. But what bothered her most was that Justin and Garrett got to attend Summit Lake Prom.

The lake rules were you had to be in high school to attend. The prom wasn't anything fancy, but Lexi couldn't wait until she was old enough. She'd spent many years listening to the music and laughter that floated up the lake from the chalet and through the open window of the loft long after she should have been asleep. From what she knew, the music was provided by an iPod, and dressing up was optional, but she didn't care. Going to the prom meant she couldn't be considered a baby, and in her best daydream, it meant a chance to kiss Justin.

Unfortunately, minutes after Lexi and Justin took the photo at the bonfire, Garrett and Angela returned from closing their cabin. Garrett grabbed a seat next to Justin, and within ten minutes, he'd convinced him to go to the point. Angela jumped up too. A year older, Angela was allowed to do more than Lexi; she could also follow Garrett around. It was the only time Lexi wished she had an older sibling. Even though Justin knew Lexi wouldn't be able to go to the point, he was nice enough to invite her. And he was right; Lexi's mom knew Angela was going, but she still thought Lexi was too little. She promised Lexi she could go next year.

Natalie backed away from the board and reached for Justin's waist. Her arm slipped around it easily, and Justin leaned into her dropping his arm around her shoulders; it caught Lexi off guard. She was suddenly very aware of the silence that'd dropped over their conversation; it was so different from the moment she'd had with Justin only minutes before. The speed of her thoughts, insecurities, and questions left her unable to break the awkwardness.

"So…" Natalie took a deep breath. "Yeah, you might get the chance to beat me." Natalie gave Justin a knowing squeeze. Lexi recognized it was Natalie's hint to Justin that she wanted to leave. Embarrassed, Lexi tried to regain her composure.

"Oh, no, you don't need to worry about me. It's Angela. If you're able to stay, she's the one you'll have to look out for. Working at the chalet she's had a lot of practice. Did you know Garrett is working there too?" Lexi focused her attention on Justin.

"Yeah, we saw them yesterday when we arrived." In her moment of panic, Lexi had forgotten about Angela's run in with them. She couldn't wait to talk to Angela about all this. What was this? Was she making things up? Did she have a moment with Justin? She was so confused. She liked him so much. What if she was wrong? After all, Justin had a girlfriend, a girlfriend he currently had his arm wrapped around. Her anxiety had pushed her stomach into her mouth, and she was worried it was about to come out.

"Ahhh! Get out, Yoga! Get out!" Lexi pushed past Justin and Natalie in an effort to prevent a very happy, wet golden retriever from shaking dry inside the cabin, but it was too late; a decades-old tennis ball dropped from the dog's mouth as he stood anxiously waiting for Lexi to throw it.

"Hi, Yoga! Still dropping in unexpected, I see." Justin bent to grab the ball. "Looks like he wants you to throw it."

"Out, Yoga!" Lexi threw the ball out the cabin door; it bounced down the granite slope a few times before hitting the shore of the lake. Yoga belonged to the Nelsons; their cabin was next to Lexi's, but it wasn't uncommon for him to drop in if he was looking for someone to play fetch with. Yoga didn't care who you were as long as you could throw.

"All right, we better get going." Justin and Natalie's arms slipped from around each other and came to their sides. Lexi watched their hands grab for one another.

"Sure, talk to you guys later." Lexi followed them to the deck. She watched them playfully bounce into each other and giggle as they headed toward Justin's cabin. She saw her sunglasses on the armrest of one of the deck chairs; putting them on, she stared out at the lake. The view never changed. It was beautiful. She saw her dad, the rainbow sail of the sunfish bright even with her glasses on. Because the lake was only a half-mile across, if her dad was watching, he'd see her wave, but he beat her and waved first. She waved back and started the short walk to the shore. Maybe a quick sail wouldn't be so bad; she could definitely use the distraction.

CHAPTER 8
LEFT BEHIND

"You want to go?" Lexi's dad shouted from the middle of the lake. It was an easy enough question, but it was hard for Lexi to answer. What she wanted was to hang out with Justin. She'd spent the last few months imagining such a different summer than what was playing out, especially the final days before the trip. She'd taken such care picking the clothes she packed. Usually, it took her about fifteen minutes to throw everything into her faded canvas bag. She packed the same clothes, shoes, and Ziploc of toiletries year after year, only changing things out as she grew, but even then it was only a pair of shorts or pants that were replaced. Her shirts were usually worn and oversized, and her go-to sweatshirt was one her dad wore in college. She liked it because it didn't have a hood, which meant she could sleep in it without getting a kink in her neck. She'd worn the same shirts for over three years. Nothing was fitted and everything had at least one stain on it. The clothes were perfect for Summit; she could hike, climb, sit on a wood railing, or slide down a rock and not worry about ruining something. They were functional but far from cute. But instead of Lexi taking minutes to pack, the hope of Justin falling for her meant she took over an hour.

She'd stood in front of her mirror, trying on each shirt and practicing hellos. Each imagined scenario came with a different one. In one, she'd planned to run her fingers through her hair, cock her head, and give a shy smile. In another, she'd flash a quick smile and say hi, maybe even give him a hug. Or she'd play it cool with just a wave. She never imagined she'd have to say hi to Justin's girlfriend.

She'd packed being careful to look good but not stand out. Her go-to look at school was jeans, a T-shirt, and Converse, but at the lake something as simple as a pair of shorts that weren't cut-offs seemed overdressed. In the end, she decided she'd risk a few of her favorite shirts. Besides, most of them were hand-me-downs from her next-door neighbor, who'd cleaned out her closet when she went away to college last year and invited Lexi to look through the boxes before they went to the Goodwill. She'd found six shirts, a pair of jeans, and a flannel, all of which were a little big but not enough to bother Lexi. The flannel was her favorite. It wasn't something she would have picked out; it had too much brown, but it was soft and perfectly faded. That's what she liked most about secondhand clothes—they gave her the courage to wear things she'd normally never try on, knowing someone else had bought and worn the piece made it safe.

"I'll go!" Lexi yelled through her cupped hands. The boats leaped and pulled against their lines. The wind had picked up, and Lexi's dad had caught a steady gust enabling him to head to the dock quickly. Lexi caught the boom as her dad pulled the sail down.

"Did you want to go by yourself?" her dad asked. From the dock, Lexi looked down at her dad. She knew he wanted her to go with him, and it'd be hard to use her usual excuses for turning him down. She knew the boat was too small to fit both of them comfortably, but with a strong wind, it could move easily through the water even under both their weights.

Lexi reached for the mast and stepped in; the boat took a dramatic dip to the left before she centered herself. She lowered into a seat, her knees and feet fighting for space between her dad's. When she was little, she'd sit between his legs, and they'd race back and forth across the lake, only coming in when Lexi's teeth had chattered far longer than her dad was comfortable with. She didn't remember being cold, only being upset that her dad didn't believe her when she'd tell him she wasn't.

The wind pushed the boat downwind from the dock as Lexi and her dad worked to raise the sail and tighten the lines. They worked in silence and in sync. There wasn't a need for directions or reminders; sailing was as much a part of the lake as kayaking or canoeing, and it was only a few seconds before the sail filled and they found their course.

"Hey, this is nice, you and me sailing. It's been a while. Thanks for coming out," her dad said.

"Sure." Lexi kept her eyes forward and readjusted her baseball cap as the wind tugged at its bill. She only wore hats at the lake, and she'd forgotten how annoying it was that her sunglasses hit the brim.

The speed of the boat knocked their knees against each other, and her dad's sandal rested on top of hers without stepping on her toes. It shouldn't have bothered her, but it did. It was an awkward feeling to be crammed into a sailboat with her dad. The boat wasn't made for two adults. The boat wasn't made for a grown daughter and her dad. She'd outgrown this.

She looked behind her at their cabin that'd shrunk with the distance they'd made. From the middle of the lake, she could easily see the five cabins that surrounded theirs. Dogs were running between them, and two of the Erickson's kids were carrying a paddleboard down the slope. She couldn't tell if it was Jacey, Emmy, Grace, or Ryan, but their fire-red hair told her they were part of the Erickson family.

"OK, ready to come about?" Her dad's voice broke her gaze, and she turned forward. The curved shore of Mermaid Cove was directly ahead. The buoy that marked the shallow waters was also the turnaround point.

As the boom swung across the boat, Lexi ducked and pulled the lines tight to fill the sail. Her dad adjusted the rudder and set their course for the cabin. Although the wind was strong, the gusts at the lake were unpredictable. Just as quickly as the sail had filled, the wind dropped, and they were stuck only to watch the sail luff in the now barely noticeable breeze.

"We had a good run," her dad said.

Lexi looked at her dad; his smile was still there familiar and comforting, but she saw something new in his face. The creases around his mouth and lines that crept from his eyes were deeper and reached farther. Maybe the mix of afternoon sun and sunscreen highlighted them, but that didn't matter; the wrinkles were there. His eyes also held a touch of sadness. She realized his words were speaking more about their sailing together than the loss of wind.

"Thanks for coming out with me. We should probably call it a day; the wind seems to be dying off, and I have a few things I need to help your uncle with. The water heater's been acting up."

The discomfort Lexi had felt earlier was fading into a feeling of bittersweet. It was one thing for her to feel like she'd outgrown something; it was another to receive confirmation from her dad.

"I'm proud of you, Lexi." Her dad's hand left the rudder and reached for her shoulder. With a squeeze of comfort, he said, "I love you."

"Thanks. I love you too, Dad." Lexi was used to her dad saying "I love you" out of the blue; it was his usual way of telling her, but in this moment, it meant more. Lexi wasn't close with her dad; he traveled a lot for work, and she grew up sharing her secrets with her mom. But at the lake, things were different; he was able to unplug and unwind something he couldn't do at home, even on weekends. His words were his way of telling her it was OK, that he knew she'd outgrown sailing with him, but that he'd be OK.

"This was fun." Lexi wanted to reassure her dad that it wasn't the activity that mattered, but the time they had. She was growing up, but she'd never stop loving him. She knew that no matter her age, she would always be his little girl, and she could live with that.

Haley was waiting for them on the dock. "Can I go?" Haley's excitement was an easy excuse for Lexi's dad to take another trip around the lake.

"Sure," Lexi's dad said. "Lexi, can you go tell your uncle I'll help him with the heater after I take Haley sailing?"

"No problem. Thanks again, Dad. Have fun, Haley."

Lexi helped push the boat away from the dock. She watched as Haley sat easily between her dad's knees and reached for the rudder; she had a huge smile on her face, and when Lexi's dad looked back to check that the rudder was free from ropes, he caught Lexi watching.

"I think she's got it," he called and gave Lexi a quick, knowing wave before he turned around.

Lexi waved back; she watched for another moment and then turned toward the cabin. Her mom waved from the deck.

"How was it?" she yelled.

Lexi reached the deck before responding, "It was fun."

"Looked a bit tight, though." Her mom laughed. "Might be the last summer you guys sail together. I was surprised you made it across the lake; it made for good watching."

"You saw that?"

"It was pretty easy to see." She turned her gaze from the lake to Lexi. "I bet you made your dad happy, though."

"Yeah." Lexi knew her mom understood. Her mom just got her. Lexi didn't have to tell her about the conversation she'd had with her dad, nor did she want to.

"He loves you so much," her mom said.

Lexi looked at her and smiled. "I know," she said.

"Of course, it's not as much as I do." Lexi's mom reached playfully for Lexi's stomach and tried to tickle her as Lexi pushed her hands back.

"I know, Mom. I love you too."

Lexi's mom relaxed back into her book, and Lexi stared across the lake at Flagpole as it sat in half shadow. The sun was hot overhead. She could feel it on her feet, the one place she was forever forgetting to wear sunscreen. She slipped one foot out of her flip-flop and examined the thin band of white that wrapped her foot. She wore her yearly flip-flop tan like a badge of honor. She saw the Ericksons and their red hair diving off their dock, swimming back, and diving again. Justin's little sister, Ellie, was with them trying to balance herself on the paddleboard that was in constant rotation between the cabins. She could see her dad and Haley across the lake and remembered she needed to remind her uncle that her dad could help him when he got back from sailing.

"Do you know where Uncle JR is?" Lexi asked.

"I think he went down to the chalet. We're out of milk, and he wanted to pick up the paper. What do you need?"

"Dad wanted me to let him know he'd help with the water heater after sailing, but I think I'm going to row over to Angela's. Can you let him know if I'm not back before he gets here?"

"No problem, honey. Have fun. Tell the Hashtacks hi for me."

"Will do. Thanks, Mom."

Lexi followed her regular path to her kayak. She knew every crack, drop, and shrub along the way. The path wasn't marked or worn-down from use; the granite looked the same as it always had, but Lexi had walked it so many times that she could do it with her eyes closed. Like most things at the lake, she'd done them since before she could remember.

From the dock she looked into her kayak. Her stomach dropped at the sight of a girl's hat tucked into the side compartment next to the seat. She knew it was Natalie's. With a defeated exhale and an eye roll, she decided she'd wait until later to return it. All she wanted now was to get away, to forget about Justin, and to take a second to be alone for the first time since she'd arrived. Her family's cabin was constantly filled with noise of family and friends, even at night. The creak of the bathroom door would fill the silence night brought and wake her. On the lake in her kayak, she got her moment to breathe. She paddled until she was in the middle and then sat with her paddle out of the water resting across her lap. She was only a couple of hundred yards from Angela's cabin, but she needed that moment to herself. After a deep breath, she started again, and a couple of minutes later, she was at the Hashtacks' dock. She looked up and caught Garrett walking onto the deck.

"Hey, Lexi!" She could always count on Garrett to make her smile. He always had a joke and genuinely enjoyed people. He was someone you wanted to be around.

"Hi, Garrett. How goes it? Is Angela around?"

"Nah, she's working at the chalet until close today."

"Oh. OK. Thanks." Lexi, who'd yet to tie up, turned back to her kayak ready to leave.

"Hey, wait! You want to come up? We're up here playing washers. You could rotate in."

Last year, if Angela hadn't been there, Lexi would have politely declined the invite, but between Garrett's enthusiasm and her need to forget Justin, she couldn't turn him down.

"Sure! Be there in a minute."

As she bent to secure her kayak, she couldn't help but feel a little excitement. Her friend's older brother wanted to hang out with her, and it didn't matter that his sister wasn't there. That was a first, and it felt pretty good.

CHAPTER 9
A MOMENT ALONE

Lexi followed the clink of the washers and laughter up hill to the back of the cabin. She recognized most of the people who sat on the deck railing and lawn chairs. The different sides of the lake were like different blocks in a neighborhood. You might not know everyone personally, but you've heard of them or seen them around. She knew Garrett and his friend Nate. She also saw Michelle and Shannon; they were a few years older than her. It'd been a while since she'd seen them, but she vividly remembered playing hide-and-seek with them when she'd paddle over to see Angela. She didn't know the other three, two guys and a girl. They stood at one end of the washer pit in deep discussions as to which washer was closest to the hole.

"That's four points for us!" one of the guys yelled as he pointed at Garrett. To win a game, a team needed twenty-one points. Each washer that made it in earned a team three points, and they'd earn an additional point for each washer that'd gotten close, as long as another team's wasn't closer. At the lake, Lexi's dad always carried a baby tape measure in his pocket. He loved being brought in to make the final decision when it was too close to call.

"Awesome!" Garrett yelled back. "We only need eight more for the win!" The three people Lexi didn't know collected the washers and walked them to their teammates. "Hey, do you guys know Lexi from the Sterling cabin? Lexi, this is Alex, Dan, and Alison. They're from the upper lake. Angela and I work with them at the chalet."

"Hey. Nice to meet you guys." Lexi smiled. Justin wasn't around; there was no Natalie, and Garrett was happy to introduce her. She was already enjoying herself. "Wait. Are you Alex Faller?" Lexi thought she'd remembered her dad talking about the Fallers. He'd helped the Fallers down from the upper lake once when the channel had gotten too low to get a boat with a motor through. Her dad had heard about their situation at the chalet and had offered to lend a hand.

"That's me." Alex smiled. "Don't tell me." He pointed at Lexi with his eyebrows raised questioning. With a smile, he asked, "Your dad is the one who helped us when we got stuck last year?"

"That was my dad."

"He totally saved us. It was much appreciated. Tell him thanks again for me. He was awesome."

"Will do! Glad everything worked out." Lexi's insecurities were gone. She felt like herself. Garrett's friends seemed nice, and he hadn't made a big deal about including her. There wasn't any mention of her being his sister's friend; he didn't bring up anything embarrassing from when they were young, and he wasn't giving her a hard time. He was being a friend, her friend.

Garrett dug into an ice chest and asked Lexi if she wanted a soda. Lexi didn't drink a lot of soda at home, but at the lake it was different. She didn't know if it was because the cabin refrigerator was unusually cold and made them taste better or if she just liked accepting one whenever she was asked. Whatever the reason, she didn't care.

"Sure. Thanks." Just as she'd caught the can Garrett threw, she heard a familiar voice.

"Lexi!" Angela was home from her job at the chalet and was excited to see her.

"Angela!" Lexi stood and hugged her.

Lexi's arms wrapped around Angela's neck. As Lexi squeezed her tight, Angela whispered into her ear. "Justin's here," she said, "with Natalie."

Even in a whisper, the news was delivered with excitement. She wanted to hang out with Justin, and this was a safe enough place to do that. It was a group setting; she was already having fun, but she was caught between wanting to hang out like they'd used to and wanting to avoid seeing Justin with someone else.

Before Lexi could let go of Angela or ask any questions, Justin and Natalie turned the corner onto the back deck. Lexi whispered, "Crap." And slowly released Angela.

"Dude! Justin. Yes! You need to play next round." Garrett was happy to have his usual teammate back.

With Angela's back to Justin, she mouthed the words "Oh my God" to Lexi. Soon Lexi's hand was in Angela's, and she was being pulled to the front of the cabin.

"Now's your chance to hang out with him." Angela's eyes sparkled at the possibilities Justin's presence meant for her friend.

"Angela, he has a girlfriend. Worse yet, he's here with her."

"I know that, but don't you want to see if maybe he has feelings for you?" There was a pleading in Angela's voice. "Think about it; you only ever get together at the lake. Makes sense that he'd have a girlfriend during the off season, but he's here now."

"I don't want to be that girl who inserts herself into other people's relationships. Does his having a girlfriend totally suck? Yes! But I'm not about to do anything crazy."

"I'm not talking crazy. Maybe just accidentally push him into a boat and drive off? Oh, come on; you know I'm kidding. All you need is a few minutes alone, to be yourself. He likes you, Lexi; he just doesn't know what that means. You're at different schools;

you're younger. I mean, you're just starting high school. Tell me you've noticed that he treats you differently. Flirts with you a little more. Finds ways to rest his arm on your shoulder, with some ridiculous excuse about you making a great arm rest because you're short."

Angela was feeding Lexi's fantasies. "That was last summer. I've barely talked to him this year."

"Whatever. It's so obvious! Are you his girlfriend? No. Does he have a crush on you? Yes!"

Lexi didn't know what to do; Angela had a habit of making a big deal out of very small things, but the possibility that Justin had a crush on her caused her heart to race, and the faster heartbeat woke the butterflies at the bottom of her stomach.

Lexi needed a second to breath, to collect her thoughts, and to decide what to do. She didn't want to leave the party; that might look weird, and plus, she was having a great time. Then she remembered she could excuse herself to grab Natalie's hat.

"Angela, I need a minute. Natalie left her hat in my boat; I'm going to grab it. It will give me a second to think."

"Perfect, I'll tell Justin to go with you."

"What? No. Just give me a minute."

Lexi looked behind her; for a moment she considered giving Angela the OK, but thought better of it. Justin and Natalie had chosen to sit on a side railing. From there they could see both the back and the front of the cabin. She didn't want Angela to make Justin go, but maybe if she walked really slow, Justin would see her and come on his own. She set her sights on her kayak and put one very slow step in front of another and hoped for a miracle.

"Wait, Lexi! Where are you going?" Justin's yell heated her cheeks.

"Oh." She turned toward them, hoping the blush wasn't obvious. "Natalie left her hat in my kayak. I wanted to grab it before I forgot."

"Awesome!" Natalie called. "I was wondering where that went. Thanks."

"Here, let me go with you." Justin was already off the railing.

Her wish came true; Lexi was going to throw up. "No, it's fine. I can get it." She couldn't believe what she was saying. But she didn't know how to be alone with him and not worry about Natalie. She didn't like that Justin had a girlfriend, but she respected it. Why did Angela have to add to the what ifs swirling in her brain.

What if there had been a strange silence between them at her cabin? What if what Angela said was true, and what if Justin wanted to be alone with her? This might be his chance. This possibility was almost too much; she knew her feelings for Justin, and guessing on his just caused her stomach to ache.

Justin ignored her refusal and caught up with Lexi before she'd made it off the deck. "I'll walk you down."

She reminded herself that walking with him didn't mean anything. The problem was she wanted it to mean everything, and she was pretty sure she was horrible at hiding it. She wondered how'd she make it down the dock.

Facing downhill, he yelled back to Natalie, "I'll be right back."

Lexi led the way. She could feel him behind her and imagined him feeling as giddy as she was. She knew this was crazy, but the idea of it lightened her steps, and they fell into a casual walk, allowing them to be side by side. Occasionally, their hands bounced off each other's on the narrow trail.

"Always trying to hold hands with me." Justin made Lexi laugh.

"I'm pretty sure it was the other way around." Lexi smiled.

Even with the awkward laughter, her heart encouraged her to keep the slow pace, because finally they were alone.

"Hey, thanks again for letting Natalie borrow your kayak."

"Sure. No problem."

The heat behind her cheeks flared again, and she hoped it wasn't enough to turn them noticeably red. Alone with him, she couldn't keep the butterflies from circling. She tried to remind herself that they were just grabbing a hat, his girlfriend's hat. But those feelings in her stomach, the excitement, the nerves, the hope—she couldn't help it. Her emotions pulled away from her logic, and she followed. Time alone—it was what her daydreams had been filled with; she wanted the world around them to stop, and then nothing would matter but them. All she'd wanted was a chance, and this was it.

"How long have you and Natalie been dating?" Her inside voice screamed for her to stop. Her one opportunity and she asked about the girlfriend. "She seems nice." She was blowing it. Lexi searched her mind for something else to talk about, but she couldn't get away from Natalie. It was Natalie's hat they were getting, it was Natalie he was introducing to the group, it was Natalie who had her arm around him, it was Natalie who was ruining Lexi's summer. It didn't matter how badly she wanted things to be different; Natalie was Justin's girlfriend, and Lexi was his friend. Friends ask about girlfriends; they don't act like girlfriends.

Justin looked down. "A couple of months." He directed his gaze toward the lake. He was wearing board shorts, a faded Summit Lake shirt, and his USC baseball cap. She remembered that shirt. She'd been at the chalet when Justin's dad had bought it for him. It was always better to buy shirts early in the season; if you waited until the end of summer, most styles were gone, and there were only a few sizes in the shirts that were left. Justin's shirt was two years old; his dad had convinced him to buy it big, so he could wear it more than one season. Two years later, the black shirt had faded to gray and fit him perfectly.

Despite Lexi's attempt at stalling, they'd reached the kayak in just a few minutes. Justin bent to grab the hat and asked, "What have you been up to?" He stood and looked at Lexi. "It's been a while." He smiled. "How are you?" He caught her off guard. She'd expected him to turn back as soon as he had the hat in his hands; instead he waited at the water's edge for her reply. She couldn't think clearly. She knew she needed to say something to keep him there.

"Good." She saw her smile reflected in his sunglasses. Something in the way he asked relaxed her. She used the calm to collect her thoughts; this was her second chance to get the conversation right. "I start high school this year."

"That's what my grandpa said. You excited?" Justin turned back to the cabin and started walking. Lexi's heart sank. That was it; that was all the alone time she'd have with him. The butterflies that'd excitedly circled her stomach only a few moments before were turning to stone. The disappointment was heavy in her gut as she turned to follow Justin up the hill.

Unlike Lexi's side of the lake, this side's shoreline was scattered with large boulders. When she was little, Angela and she would sit on them and watch the chipmunks dart in and out of the nests they'd created underneath the large granite stones.

"Kinda." Lexi just missed stepping on the back of Justin's heal. He'd stopped suddenly in front of a boulder, and with her head hung, Lexi hadn't noticed.

"About what?" He turned toward Lexi and reached back for the boulder and hopped up. The boulder was big enough for Lexi to sit next to him, but there wouldn't be much room between them if she did. She felt weird joining him, so she stood.

"I don't know?" She looked over his shoulder. She could see Angela, Garrett, Natalie, and the others throwing washers.

Justin laughed. "So you're excited but don't know what for?" He took his sunglasses off to rub his eyes.

Lexi felt that familiar heat in her cheeks. "I don't know. I guess it will be nice to have a change." His eyes smiled, and she caught a glimpse of his one dimple. She couldn't look away from him. "Plus doesn't being in high school make you super cool?"

"Oh. Way cool." He kept his focus on Lexi. "But I wouldn't know. I was pretty cool before I started."

He winked, and Lexi smiled. "That's right; I forgot," she said.

CHAPTER 10

THE UNEXPECTED

Lexi took a deep breath; even in the moment, she felt it. Her brain was gathering each detail significant or not. Her brain slowed the conversation; it needed the extra time to seal the experience into memory. Every color, sound, smell, and feeling filed in neat and clean in order to be locked and secured. Each second was important, but while her brain worked to slow and sort, her emotions rushed, and she felt like she was falling.

To anyone watching it was an ordinary, insignificant conversation, and Lexi knew that's how she had to treat it, that's how it needed to look, that's how she'd make it look. Justin was an old friend; he had a girlfriend just up the hill, and she told herself she was mature enough to keep it together.

Lexi's hands nervously tucked her hair away from her face, and she pulled at her jean shorts. She'd rushed cutting them from an old pair of jeans, and the right side always felt higher. She also felt awkward in her stance. She faced uphill and couldn't get her footing right, and when she did, her chest became even with Justin's eyes, which meant the uncomfortable fidgeting would start again.

"Hard to believe we're both in high school," Justin said. His eye contact caused Lexi to shift her weight back and forth. She'd hold it as long as she could, before she'd look at her feet. She'd painted her toes a bright watermelon pink before she'd left home. She thought it was a good color for summer, but the last few days had peeled the paint, and the bottoms of her toes were turning a rust color from her worn leather flip-flops that didn't have time to dry between dips in the lake. From her feet, back to his eyes, then her feet again. It hurt to look at him; it caused too many feelings.

But Lexi longed to keep the conversation going, even if she couldn't maintain eye contact. She took a deep breath and released. "And you'll be in college in a year," she said. A relaxed smile started across her face. She'd done it; she'd given the conversation momentum. She steadied herself as her anxiety started to fade. They'd fallen into a light topic she could easily talk about and was encouraged that Justin had decided to sit. She decided that it meant he wanted more time, more time with her. She could do this, she thought. Her gaze left her feet but didn't connect with Justin's, because his had dropped.

"Maybe," he said without a hint of self-pity. The humor had left his voice. "I'm having second thoughts." He kicked at a small rock and watched it bounce down the granite until it jumped the water's edge and landed about a foot in with a louder splash than Lexi had expected. She watched his eyes follow the ripples until they smoothed. He stared at the lake, but he wasn't looking at it; he was lost in his thoughts.

"Did you get it?" Natalie called from above as she leaned over the deck railing.

Justin dropped his head and looked at his hand that held his mirrored sunglasses before he put them on. Instead of looking into his eyes, Lexi was left with a reflection of herself, but the image didn't bring insecurities; she was too focused on Justin's words. They'd caught her off guard and turned the conversation from lighthearted to confusing. He'd always wanted to go to college, and Lexi was worried to hear otherwise.

She felt caught. Natalie had interrupted them before she had time to react to what Justin had said. Lexi had made every attempt to keep her cool and act as friend like as possible. She didn't want to give Natalie any reason to question why it was taking so long, but Justin's confession had dropped her guard, and Lexi reached for his shoulder; he stood before she touched it.

"Got it!" he yelled. He'd already turned from Lexi and was headed for Natalie.

"Wait!" Her words and thoughts tangled together letting only one word out at a time. "What?" Lexi was confused. "Stop!" He didn't slow. She needed more time with him. His confession shook her out of her flirtation and immediately put her into friend mode. Not the kind of friend that hopes to be more, but the kind who's there regardless.

"Forget it," he said without looking back. "It's nothing. I'm probably just nervous. Don't worry about it."

"Of course you'll get in." Lexi scrambled to make light of things. They didn't have time for a serious conversation. "I mean, why wouldn't they want you? I mean, you're super cool." She hated her immature response, but it was all she could come up with feeling like a little kid as she followed behind him. Two questions ran through her mind; the first was why had Justin told her, and the second, more important, was when would she have a chance to talk to him.

Lexi felt awkward from the moment they stepped back onto the deck. Justin hadn't said it, but she guessed she knew something Natalie didn't. Lexi also knew Justin well enough to know when he wanted things kept quiet. There'd been more than a few occasions when Lexi and Justin had found themselves alone after Angela and Garrett had gone home and the adults from their cabins would laugh and talk out on the back deck, reminiscing. Lexi and Justin would sit inside, tell ghost stories, and finish the chocolate from the s'mores they'd already had too many of.

Justin was fifteen when he told Lexi he didn't like the dark. She laughed and asked if he was more worried about ghosts or zombies. He laughed along with her and then quieted and tried to explain his unease. He said the worst was twilight, when the sun was gone from view, but it was light enough to see silhouettes against the gray of the sky. He told her it was a lonely feeling; the day was turning off, and so was everything in it. It was when friends went home, things closed, and the sound turned down. Once the black of night filled in the gray, the silhouettes became invisible and the dark settled; there was nothing to see, nothing to do, and it meant the routine of sleep would be only hours away, and, for him, it never came easy.

At almost thirteen, Lexi felt the weight of his thoughts and felt honored that he'd shared them with her. There was the small part of her that questioned why'd he feel safe telling her, but the larger part of her reveled in the idea that whatever the reason for his confession he chose her and that meant something. Neither of them brought it up again. Lexi knew it was one of those rare moments that would diminish with each retelling, so it was a conversation she kept tucked away until she needed fuel for her daydreams.

Then last year, on the night of the Summit Lake Prom, Lexi's mom was making Lexi's favorite double-chocolate brownies when she asked Lexi to get more chocolate chips from the chalet. Turned out, Haley had used them trying to catch fish. Her mom hoped the brownies would help Lexi feel better about being too young to go to the prom. Lexi was halfway down the rocks when Justin called to her from above, "Can I catch a ride?"

She turned to see Justin in a fitted black suit, paired with a faded Hawaiian shirt and bow tie. On anyone else it would have looked ridiculous, but on Justin, Lexi thought it was perfection.

"What do you think?" Justin asked as he walked off his deck with his arms extended toward Lexi on the dock.

"I think the shirt makes the outfit." Lexi couldn't help but smile. It was a mix of colors, but purple and orange dominated the flowery patterned fabric. As he got closer, she recognized it as one of Mr. Roberts's. No matter the temperature, Mr. Roberts wore a Hawaiian shirt. The Roberts family had a second home on Maui; Lexi's family had visited once when she was little, but she was too young to remember.

"That's what I'm saying! My grandpa loaned it to me." Justin did a quick spin, slipped, but caught himself before he went down.

"Smooth moves too." Lexi laughed, but it was bittersweet. She wanted to go with Justin, not drop him off.

"I need a ride to the chalet. Garrett's working tonight, and he's going to change there. I thought I could just meet him. Can you take me?"

"Sure," Lexi had said.

Justin untied the bowline as Lexi started the motor. He stepped in with one foot and used his other to push away from the dock. A second later he was across from Lexi, with that one-dimpled smile.

"It stinks that you can't go," he said.

"I know," Lexi had said without looking at him. "One more year." The last word caught in her throat as unexpected tears pooled in her eyes. The hum of the motor hid the sound of her disappointment, and the wind held the tears back.

A few minutes before the chalet, Justin broke the sullen silence. "I think Michelle is going to be there," he said. "I wish she wasn't. I've heard from a few people that she likes me, but the feeling isn't mutual. What do you think I should do?" The question pulled Lexi from her disappointment. His interest in her advice made her feel special. She didn't have much of an answer, but it was enough that he'd asked. Confessions, questions about love, moments of honesty, shared concerns, and his visible emotions were what fed Lexi's feelings for him. She was certain he liked being alone with her, and for her the feeling was mutual.

Natalie approached them and thanked Lexi for remembering her hat. Once Justin had replaced the hat on Natalie's head,

Natalie popped onto her tiptoes and gave Justin a quick kiss on his lips. Only an hour before, Lexi's stomach would have turned, but it was different now. She didn't have to question her connection to him; he'd done what he always had. It'd been brief, but he was still reaching for her, even if he wasn't reaching for her hand. The confidence Lexi felt wasn't diluted with hope; Justin's actions had given her a solid footing.

"Lexi, you're up." Angela held out four washers for Lexi.

"Thanks, but I think I'm going to head back." Lexi wanted a simple out and didn't care if it was believable or not. She didn't have the energy. "I just remembered…" She caught a skeptical look from Angela. "I promised to help my mom with some stuff. See you guys later."

CHAPTER 11

IT WILL WORK OUT

Lexi hadn't promised her mom anything, but since she'd used her as an excuse, she felt an obligation to ask her mom if she needed help. Her honesty often got in the way; once she'd found twenty dollars in the locker hallway at school, and instead of considering herself lucky, she turned it into the office thinking someone might come looking for it.

Given the heat and time of day, she guessed her mom had moved inside. The cabin provided a break from the sun. Sunglasses could come off, and there were fewer bugs. An occasional fly would pass through the almost always open front door, bang against the large picture window with the view of the lake, change course, and then continue toward the kitchen and out the back. If Lexi had to pick one thing at the lake to complain about, it was the bugs. The sound of the flies that seemed perpetually lost in a series of circles and the nightly return of mosquitoes sent Lexi looking for shelter and bug spray. The mosquitoes were the worst; their bites left her with unusually swollen, hot, itchy patches that could take over a week to heal, sometimes leaving scars. Angela still laughs about the time Lexi was bitten on her forehead; it was right in the middle and swelled to the size of a golf ball. She'd thought she was safe with everything covered and her hood pulled tight over her head, but the little bit of forehead that showed was too irresistible.

She found her mom reading at the kitchen table; her back against the cabin wall, and her legs stretched out along the table bench. It was heavy and solid, and Lexi hit her knee on it almost every other day. It seemed an odd place to cozy up with a book. "What are you doing?" Lexi asked her mom. "You can't be comfortable."

"I've had it with that couch," her mom said. She set her book face down to hold her place. "I feel like I have to work to sit on it; it's awful." Her mom rolled her eyes, shook her head in frustration, and refocused. "You're back early. What's up?" she asked. "How's Angela?"

"She's OK," Lexi said.

For a moment she considered telling her mom about Justin. She shared a lot with her mom, but her mom had a habit of putting things into perspective, which meant Lexi usually left their conversations feeling disappointed. It wasn't like talking to her friends. When she talked to her friends about a crush, they'd delight in the possibilities and encourage her to examine every detail of her interactions with him for proof of a shared attraction. But her mom called it like she saw it, and if Lexi mentioned her frustration with Natalie or Justin's hesitation about college, her mom would most likely remind Lexi that it wasn't her business and to stay out of it. But Lexi wanted Justin to be her business, and she wasn't ready to hear otherwise; she kept her mouth shut. Besides, she couldn't shake the feeling that Justin wanted her involved.

"I was wondering if you needed help with anything?" Lexi asked. She mentally crossed her fingers hoping the answer was no. "I know Grandma mentioned something about touching up the trim around the windows."

Painting the trim was a safe suggestion; like the couch, it was discussed every year without follow-through. If they'd started painting it when it was first mentioned, it could have already been painted three times over. But no one could agree on a color, a stain, or the right person for the job, just that it needed to be done. The problem was cabin improvements were easy to talk about during the off-season, because the cabin seemed a world away, but once summer came, all anyone wanted was to enjoy the cabin. The work could wait.

"I still don't think we've decided on a color," her mom said with another frustrated shake of her head. "If you're really looking for something to do, you could go next door and ask Nancy if she wants help. She dropped by earlier and mentioned she's organizing the songbooks for the Summit Lake Day BBQ. She'd probably love an extra hand."

"Cool. Thanks." Lexi headed out the back door. Nancy was Justin's mom. Being neighbors, she'd helped her many times; usually it was with Justin. The worst was when they had to disinfect the kazoos that were passed around each year. Unfortunately, that year they'd been unintentionally collected in a plastic bag that'd been used for potato salad and sealed. Three days went by before Nancy got to them. As if the smell of the salad wasn't bad enough, the amount of spit that dripped from the kazoos was enough to fill a jug. It didn't matter how much she enjoyed hanging out with Justin, she hadn't volunteered to help him with that job since.

"Hello?" Lexi yelled into the Robertses' cabin as she stepped inside. The familiar colors of avocado green and mustard yellow, a lingering smell of smoke from the stone fireplace, and the faded book spines that lined the shelf next to the window warmed the place in Lexi's heart reserved for things that felt like home. It'd always looked this way, and she hoped it'd never change. Mr. Roberts, Justin's grandpa, had bought the cabin in the midsixties. He and Justin's grandma, Eloise, filled the cabin with books about the mountain ranges, wild flowers, and histories of the lake. The cabin's furniture was well loved and put to good use even before it settled in the cabin, and the newest piece of kitchen equipment was a glass baking dish that'd been left at one of the potlucks and was never claimed. The only pieces added over the years were a few of Eloise's beautiful oil paintings she'd painted from their dock and the collection of Summit Lake Day awards that hung from the rafters.

"Anyone here?" Lexi called before her eye caught something on the mantel. There wedged between a bottle of sunscreen and bug spray sat the picture Justin had pocketed of her and him at last year's bonfire. It hurt her to see it there. It felt like it'd been discarded; she couldn't let it stay like that. Delicately, she removed the picture, taking a moment to look at it closely for the millionth time. They were both wearing beanies and down jackets. As hot as the days were, the temperature could drop drastically at night. The light of the fire had prevented the flash from going off, and although it made for a darker photograph, Lexi loved how the fire-light held them in an orange glow, shadowing everyone but them. Each time she looked at it, she hoped to see something new, some definitive proof, that told her Justin felt the same way she did. She looked hard, but she couldn't see anything. Before putting it back, she rearranged the bottles and then used a piece of driftwood to prop the picture up.

"Hi, Lexi!" Nancy came from the direction of the back dorm carrying a large cardboard box. "Sorry," she said. "I was in the back dorm going through the songbooks." Nancy pulled one out of the thirty songbooks that filled the box and four pages dropped from the middle. "They're all like this with pages missing."

"Oh, wow, that's not good." Lexi said as she bent down to pick the pages off the worn wooden floor. She shuffled them back into place and handed them to Nancy. "My mom said you might like some help."

"That would be great. Thank you." Nancy looked genuinely re-lieved at Lexi's offer. "If you could flip through the books and find which pages are missing, I can organize the loose ones, and hopefully we can get through it quickly. Once I have them in order, I'll be able to fix the bindings, and we'll be all set."

"Sure, no problem." Lexi liked Nancy, because she talked to her like an adult, which was rare on the lake. It was hard for the majority of grown-ups around the lake to recognize when someone was no longer a kid.

Together they sat cross-legged on the floor and got to work. Both the work and the conversation were easy. Nancy asked Lexi about school and her grandma, and Lexi was happy to talk. She hadn't realized until then that she'd felt like she'd been holding her breath the past few days. She asked Nancy about Justin's little sister, Ellie, and if the rumor that Mr. Roberts had fallen through the ice last winter was true, and Yoga came in more than once looking for someone to throw his ball. Then without even thinking, she said, "So what do you think about Natalie?" She couldn't help it; Justin was never far from her thoughts. Everything had been so comfortable; she hoped the question wouldn't stand out. The last thing she wanted was for Nancy to think something was up.

"You know, Natalie's nice," Nancy answered without pause. "I just don't know if she's right for Justin. I think she's very excited about having a boyfriend, and I think Justin got caught up in her excitement. Actually, I'm surprised he invited her. He'd said earlier that he was looking forward to having some space this summer while at the lake. I think she may have talked him into giving her an invitation."

Lexi didn't know how to respond. Nancy had shared this without hesitation, and she didn't think she was looking for Lexi's input. "Well..." she said, "I'm sure it will all work out."

CHAPTER 12
PUZZLE PIECES

The rain had come last night just after she'd gone to bed. She liked the rain. California saw little of it, and when it came, it changed everything. The smell, the colors in the sky, how it washed the dust away and pooled into oil-slicked puddles. When she was little, it meant games of Heads Up, Seven Up; indoor lunches; and a chance to wear rain boots and drink hot chocolate. The storms at the lake were different. In the mountains, the drops were fat, loud, and frequent. There weren't puddles of oil rainbows or umbrellas; instead thunder and lightning hit without notice and carried a beautiful violence that faded into a gentle pitter-patter.

The storm had cooled the loft, and the clouds kept the morning dark. Her eyes closed, Lexi snuggled deep into her sleeping bag. The light rhythm of the exiting rain brought her thoughts back to the night before.

After she'd finished helping Nancy, she'd come back to the makings of an early dinner. Her grandma stood at the sink washing tomatoes and didn't hear Lexi come in. Lexi watched her. She wanted to soak in the moment. She'd lost her other grandma the year before and recognized that this seemingly insignificant moment, wasn't insignificant at all. She knew her grandma wouldn't always be at that sink, and when the time came, Lexi wanted the memory of her there to be rich.

Not a second later, her grandma caught sight of her out of the corner of her eye and put Lexi to work drying. The tomatoes were beautiful; they came from her grandma's garden, and Lexi had been spoiled on them. She couldn't eat a store-bought tomato without disappointment. Tomatoes and peach-colored roses—she couldn't think of either without thinking of her grandma.

"What's for dinner?" Lexi asked. The kitchen smelled amazing, and her stomach was tugging on her insides looking for food. It was a reminder that she'd had little to eat since Justin had arrived. The anxiety of seeing him, then seeing him with Natalie, and not knowing what to say to him about college kept her stomach full. But the smell of her grandma's cooking created room. "I'm starving," she said.

"I thought we'd have tacos," her grandma said as she lifted the lid to give the seasoned ground beef a stir. "It isn't fancy, but I know it's something Haley will eat, and your dad is always a fan."

Lexi was a fan too. Her mom made tacos at home, but they never turned out as good as her grandma's. "Awesome! Sounds good to me." Lexi got to work, shredding the cheese. At home her family used preshredded cheese, but at the lake, cheese was shredded with a centuries-old cheese-grater. Lexi had lost count of the number of times she'd cut her knuckles while using it. Last year, she suggested they switch to the packaged stuff but was shot down by everyone. She loved that her family wanted to keep the cabin as rustic as possible, but there were some things she thought they could give on, and cheese was one of them.

Haley popped in as they were cooking and dug through the grocery bags under the table that held the snacks. "I'm hungry," she whined. Haley was still in her bathing suit, which wasn't unusual, and when she did change, it was from a wet suit to a dry one. But the air was cooling, and it was becoming a matter of when and not if the rain would come.

"Dinner is almost ready. You don't need a snack." Lexi's aunt had followed Haley into the kitchen on a motherly hunch.

"But, I'm starving!" Haley was shoulders deep into a grocery bag and barely auditable.

"You can't have a snack before dinner." Lexi had the impression that this was a regular conversation between Haley and her aunt. "Go grab some sweats and a jacket, and when you come back, we'll eat."

"What are we eating?" Haley wanted to make sure it was worth the wait.

"Tacos!" her grandma exclaimed, which sent Haley running for warmer clothes.

Lexi's family fit snugly around the table, but because they sat on picnic benches instead of chairs, it seemed less crowded. Her uncle asked her about school and if she planned to play any sports, while her aunt told stories about Haley. Haley managed to sit long enough to finish one taco before she went to work on a puzzle she'd started three days before, and soon the conversation turned to cabin projects and lake gossip, none of which was very exciting. Lexi excused herself and headed to the other room to help Haley.

The puzzle was a familiar one; she'd done it every summer, once with Justin. She knew Haley was excited to complete it but also knew it wouldn't be easy for her. The pieces were a little too small, and the picture lacked details, which made it hard to find pieces. Lexi was working on completing the boarder when there was a knock at the door. Lexi looked up and saw Justin peeking into the window with a wave. Lexi's stomach lurched, and she jumped to open the door.

"Hey." Lexi took a moment to breath. "What's up?"

"Hi, sorry. My grandpa wanted to know if we could have a couple of zip ties. He's trying to secure the tarp over our firewood."

"Sure. Come in."

"Hi, Haley." He waved. Haley didn't flinch. "I remember that puzzle." Justin walked to the coffee table, picked up a piece, and put it in. "Didn't your uncle bet us that we couldn't complete it in under an hour? He promised us ice cream from the chalet if we did it."

"Oh my God, that's right. I knew we'd put it together but forgot about the bet. We won, right?" The memory made Lexi smile.

"No, we didn't. But your aunt felt bad for us and gave us the money anyway."

It warmed Lexi's heart that Justin remembered more details about a shared experience than she did. At home, months from seeing Justin, she'd occasionally stumble across her insecurities and obsess on whether Justin thought as much about her as she thought about him. It seemed every detail, of every encounter, was burned into her memory because of the incessant replay in her head. And yet, here was a memory that he held missing pieces to. He remembered things about her, things that she didn't, things that made him laugh and smile. She wondered how many other moments he held on to, things that meant something to him that she'd missed.

"Oh, hi, Justin." Lexi's dad shook Justin's hand. "You hungry? We have plenty of leftovers if you're interested."

"No, thanks. I was just stopping by for my grandpa. My dad is teaching Natalie how to cook his famous spaghetti sauce. I was wondering if I could have a few zip ties?"

"Sure. Give me a second. I have to remember where I last used them."

Lexi's dad headed outside to the storage shed. Even if they were in there, it'd take a few minutes for him to find them. Organizing the shed was another thing on the cabin's to-do list. Lexi returned to the couch, making sure to leave an open seat. "Want to help?" she asked.

"Sure." Justin walked around the puzzle and found his seat next to Lexi. "I can't believe you don't remember that. We were so close. We were something like seven pieces from completing it. Your uncle gave us such a hard time until your aunt came in and made him stop."

"I remember doing the puzzle, just not the bet." Lexi hadn't turned her gaze from the puzzle; it was comforting to have a reason not to look up. She didn't think her stomach could handle eye contact with him this close. Lexi left enough room for him to sit without touching her, but he hadn't taken advantage of it. Instead, he slid in close. His leg rested against hers, and each time he leaned forward to grab a puzzle piece, his shoulder would brush against her arm. He'd put in four pieces, before Lexi had found one. Her eyes were on the puzzle, but she wasn't seeing it; she was only feeling him.

"You're not very good at this." Justin laughed. "No wonder we lost the bet."

"Shut up!" Lexi pushed Justin and watched as he faked her strength and fell over.

"I'm serious." Justin sat up and nudged her with his shoulder.

"I want dessert," Haley proclaimed before dropping her piece and walking back into the kitchen.

Lexi watched her go and saw her opportunity. "So about that college thing?" she asked keeping her eyes on the puzzle. "What's up with that? You've always wanted to go."

"It's not that I don't want to go; it's just weird to think I only have one year of high school left. I don't know; it's hard to explain. I tried to talk to Natalie about it, but she thinks I'm crazy. She can't wait to go away to school. I guess there's something about becoming a grown-up; I'm not all that excited about being an adult."

He took a second to consider his words and then turned toward Lexi, and she looked up. She saw it in his eyes; he needed someone to get it. She didn't have words, but she gave him a soft smile and a head nod. He returned both. Their eyes locked on one another's, and there was a tangible, comfortable innocence to the moment that left Lexi's heart floating.

"Found some!" Lexi's dad carried with him a dozen zip ties in a variety of sizes.

Justin stood to meet him and thanked him for finding them. "Good luck on the puzzle," he said as he made his way out the door.

"Thanks!" Haley said returning to the room with a tray of marshmallows, graham crackers, and chocolate.

"Have a good night, Justin." Lexi smiled.

Lexi spent the last hours before bed working on the puzzle with Haley and helping to roast s'mores. She went to bed feeling better than she had in days. Tucked into her sleeping bag, with the rain tapping the roof above, she drifted off warmed by the thought of Justin sitting next to her. She couldn't help but wonder if he was thinking about her too.

CHAPTER 13

CHANGE OF PLANS

A few days had passed since Lexi had run into Justin. She'd spent her time walking Haley back and forth from the cabin to the point, reading, and catching up with Angela. Angela's work schedule at the chalet made it hard for them to hang out as much as they had in summers past.

She missed her friend. Angela was the one person she could talk to about Justin. Angela got it; she knew Lexi and Justin's history. Lexi had tried to explain Justin to her friends back home but never felt like she succeeded. Justin was more than a crush. There was a magic to the lake that complicated things, something her friends couldn't understand. But none of that mattered today, because today was Wednesday.

Tomorrow, Natalie would find out if she'd have to return to compete in the soccer championships, and Lexi had her fingers crossed. If Natalie went home today, she'd miss the prom, the competitions, and the bonfire. Lexi wouldn't have to share any part of Summit Lake Day, and more importantly, she wouldn't have to share Justin.

She'd spent the early morning in bed praying for Natalie's departure, but eventually the increasing heat in the loft drove her out. She hadn't yet changed from her pajamas, when she slipped on her flip-flops and took her hot chocolate to the deck where she settled into the cushions of one of the many Adirondack chairs. The cabin was quiet; she figured her parents were off on their usual morning paddle and that her grandma had headed to the neighbors for a cup of coffee and chitchat. She wasn't sure where Haley was, but she was glad she didn't have to listen to her. Maybe her aunt and uncle had taken Haley and joined her parents in the canoe.

A few boats circled the lake. Someone was out on skis, and the taxi boat eased out of the channel, before gunning it back to the chalet. For all the time Lexi had spent on the lake, she'd only taken the taxi once. Those who rode were usually people without cabins—hikers who were on their way to desolation wilderness. The entrance to the trail was just past the old Scout camp. On holiday weekends, the taxi would cross the lake too many times to count. Besides the hikers, you could usually count on at least one dog, usually a lab, who looked just as excited to start the journey.

Even with all the other motors, she could hear it. For a moment, she was struck by how something so familiar could cause her such anxiety. The late-morning sun stung her eyes and brought her hand to her forehead in an effort to shade her view. She could hear the Robertses' boat but couldn't see it. She squinted hard at the lake, before she found it, and it took another second to confirm that Justin was the only one inside. The logical explanation was that he'd been fishing. She didn't blame Natalie for wanting to sleep. The prime fishing started about 5:00 a.m., and even then you weren't promised a catch.

Lexi waved, and Justin caught sight of her and waved back. As he cut the engine to tie up, he yelled good morning.

"How'd you do?" Lexi asked. "Catch anything?" There was a familiarity to the conversation; for as much as they did together, fishing was never one of them. Justin would go out, and Lexi would welcome him in, usually from her deck while drinking hot chocolate. Only once had she made it up in time to go with him, and it wasn't something she was interested in doing again.

"What?" he asked. Justin flipped his hat back to the front and made his way up from the dock.

Instead of fishing gear, he carried a half gallon of milk. Lexi started to think twice about her assumption but kept with routine. "Fishing? How was the fishing?" He didn't have an answer. "Did you go fishing?"

Justin stopped on the granite slab just in front of Lexi's deck. Seeing him up close, Lexi was certain he hadn't. "Nah. I had to take Natalie to the airport," he said without much emotion.

The closest airport to Summit is an hour away with only a couple of flights a day. When Lexi was little, she'd beg her parents to fly to Summit, hoping to avoid the drive, but they never did. The flights into and out of the airport were expensive. Lexi had asked a million times when she was little if they could fly to Summit instead of drive, but the answer was always no.

His response didn't make sense. Natalie wouldn't know if she'd be needed back home until tomorrow. "Why?" she asked. The question popped out before Lexi had a chance to refine it. "I mean, is there anything wrong? Is everyone OK?" She worked to hold her excitement at bay; she told herself she wouldn't let herself feel until she knew everyone was OK. But she'd need answers quick if she was going to keep her emotions in check. Her inner voice was fighting with her conscience as it chanted, "She's gone! She's gone! Finally, she's gone!"

"Everything's fine. We just broke up." Justin's eyes didn't fall from Lexi's. They stayed steady and sweet and complimented an awkward smile, the kind you give when you don't know what else to say. Lexi returned it.

"That stinks. I'm sorry." She was surprised by her authenticity.

"I guess her mom offered to fly her home when she called her last night. I offered to drive her back today, but something about making a four-hour drive after you've just broken up doesn't sound the greatest. To be honest, I'm glad she took the flight. I wasn't looking forward to the drive either."

"What happened?" Lexi asked.

"After I talked to you about college, I started thinking about a lot of things. I don't know; it felt weird to have a girlfriend here. I mean, the lake's always been an escape from things, and having Natalie here changed that. I tried to talk to her about why I wasn't as excited as her to leave for college, and she couldn't get it. I needed her to get it."

"That makes sense," Lexi said.

"It didn't help that my grandpa kept teasing her about passing the Summit test. He said there was a checklist of things she'd need to accomplish to be considered a true laker."

"I could totally do that." Lexi smiled hoping to lighten the mood.

Justin gave a soft laugh and shook his head. "It doesn't count if you're born into it." His smile lingered along with his gaze before he turned it toward his cabin. "Well, I should probably go put the milk in the fridge."

"Sure." Lexi was disappointed that the conversation was ending. "Hey, if you want to talk about it…"

"Nah. How about we just take the canoe out later? We'll go see what Garrett and Angela are up to. I saw Garrett at the chalet when I bought the milk, and he said they get off about three in the afternoon"

"Cool." Lexi's heart backflipped. "Sounds good."

"Awesome," he said.

"Oh…And hey." Lexi couldn't resist. "Nice hat." It was his USC hat, the one he wore in spite of his grandpa's wishes he attend his alma mater, and she loved that she knew that.

"You think?" Justin's hand instinctively reached for the bill of the cap.

"Looks good on you." Lexi's eyes twinkled.

"Thanks. I'm thinking about going to college there." He winked and started back toward his cabin. She watched him go.

"Maybe you'll get a water-polo scholarship!" she yelled.

CHAPTER 14

RAIN LIKELY

With time to kill, Lexi sipped her hot chocolate. She savored the warmth of it and enjoyed the calm it brought her. She was excited for what the afternoon would bring, but she was content to wait. Natalie's absence and the return of easy conversation with Justin gave her daydreams a foothold. She could see it, taste it even; the possibility of being with Justin was growing into probability. She thought about the prom, what she'd wear, how she'd ask him to dance, if he'd ask her to dance. What she'd say, and how the night would end in a kiss. Her heart quickened at the image but settled with another sip of her hot chocolate. A soft, knowing smile crossed her lips. She found it funny that her daydreams could be both incredibly simple and annoyingly complex. All she wanted was for Justin to like her; why did she have to make it so complicated?

"You're awake." Her grandma was both surprised and happy to find her on the porch. Lexi's grandma came to rest next to Lexi's chair and looked out onto the lake. She held her favorite coffee cup; it was handmade, the color of jade, and it had a fat handle. Her grandma needed two hands to carry it. Once when Lexi was little, her grandma let her use it; she remembered because of how special it made her feel. She'd never seen her grandma loan it to anyone. "What are your plans for the day?" her grandma asked as she set the cup on Lexi's armrest, leaving her hands free to reach for Lexi. Her fingers combed through Lexi's hair.

"Oddly enough," Lexi said, "I think I woke up because it was too quiet. It's never this quiet, especially when Haley is here."

Her grandma dropped Lexi's hair without offense, patted her on the head, and went back to her coffee. Lexi reached to tuck the fallen strands behind her right ear and turned her head toward her grandma. Each time Lexi looked at her, she'd catch a glimpse of something that reminded her that her grandma was aging. Sometimes it'd be an age spot; on other occasions, it'd be more wrinkles around her eyes. In this moment it was the skin on her grandma's arms. It was colored with small bruises. Most had already yellowed with healing, while others were dark purple. Bruises come easy with age; the skin is thinner, and it doesn't take much for one to appear. Lexi hated the constant reminders that her grandma wouldn't always be here.

"I think Justin and I are going to take the canoe over to Angela's later, but that's not until after lunch," she said. The beauty of the lake was that you didn't need to have finite plans; it was enough to sit and soak in the surroundings.

"You could go with me into town," her grandma suggested. "It's my job to pick up the fire permit at the ranger station for Saturday's bonfire." Lexi wasn't thrilled about the idea of moving. She had settled on the deck nicely, and while she adored her grandma, the idea of running errands exhausted her. "What if I throw in lunch?" her grandma offered. She sensed Lexi's hesitation and knew food could help sweeten the deal.

"OK," Lexi said, "I'm in." She couldn't say no to lunch. Besides, the more she thought about it, a trip into town would get her mind far enough from the lake to maybe think of something other than Justin.

The one-way road off the mountain was steep and winding but short. After that, it was straight highway until you hit a fork. Turn right and head farther into the mountains; turn left and you'd find a grocery store, two gas stations, five stoplights, a sporting-goods store, and a handful of small businesses, including a coffee stop, hardware store, and thrift shop.

The ranger station was nothing more than a small kiosk, with one ranger looking for something to do. It took Lexi's grandma less than five minutes to return with an illegible signed and stamped permit. "That's it? I could have signed that for you," Lexi said.

"But then we'd have missed the opportunity to have lunch together." Her grandma smiled.

Lexi was excited about lunch. The coffee stop served one of the best tuna sandwiches she'd ever had. She looked forward to it whenever they came to town around lunchtime. She didn't know if it was the cheese melted on top or the bag of plain potato chips that came with it, but there was something about the sandwich that made her happy. Most likely, it had something to do with the memories she had eating there, and there were too many to count.

After lunch, Lexi glanced at her watch; their lunch break hadn't carried them into noon, and she was disappointed that more time hadn't passed. The thrift store was next to the coffee stop and had a window display that peeked her interest, plus she could kill more time inside, so she suggested they check it out.

As she flipped through a shoebox of old postcards, the word "Summit" caught her attention. In big white letters the card read, Visit Summit Lake; the words arched over an old picture of the chalet. Lexi knew the picture had to be from the 1960s because the taxi dock wasn't in the shot, and her dad had told countless stories about helping to build it. She was certain of the dates because one of the stories included the time he had his first beer. It was on the last day of dock construction; it'd been both an early start and a late day, but they'd managed to finish before the close of the season. It was Mr. Swanson who owned the chalet then, and while her dad never had anything nice to say about working for him, he had one fond memory. It was Mr. Swanson handing him a cold beer to toast the dock's completion. Lexi's dad was only seventeen and had never had a drink before then.

She flipped the card over. "My love, you are missed by every piece of me. I'm here until September 8. Please come." It was signed, "Always yours," with the initials EJB and included a PS that read, "Don't ever forget."

The penciled plea left Lexi enchanted. She felt them; they spoke to her imagination and the hope that one day she'd have someone write those words to her. She wondered who EJB was but quickly decided to assume that EJB was a him and conjured up an image of a gorgeous guy, sitting above the lake, dreaming of his love, and desperately hoping this postcard would bring her to him. And in her mind, it did; his love received the card, responded with one of her own promising to come as soon as possible. Then, finally, after a month of written exchanges, they reconnected and greeted each other with a kiss that spoke more than words ever could.

Hoping to find more of EJB's postcards, she continued to look through the cards, but she turned the box to see the messages and not the pictures. Most read about vacations, others had bits of town gossip, and a few spoke of being homesick. The majority of them ended their cards with love, but none spoke of it the way the Summit card had. Wrapped in fantasies of past lives, Lexi managed to lose track of time. It wasn't until her grandma came up from behind and surprised her that she returned to the here and now.

"What did you find?" Lexi's grandma peeked over her shoulder at the postcard Lexi held. "Is that a picture of the chalet?" Lexi handed her grandma the card, who was quick to point out the missing dock.

"I think I'm going to buy it," Lexi told her grandma. "For history's sake." Lexi looked at her watch. It was 1:30 p.m. They'd make it back to the lake with enough time to keep Lexi anxiously waiting but not enough time to drive her patience crazy.

The ride up the mountain was quiet. Lexi leaned her forehead against the window and looked for shapes in the clouds above. They were the kind of clouds that made Lexi want to fly. As a little girl, she'd lay in her backyard and stare at the sky wishing she could touch it. The blue of the sky, the color she loved but never felt right describing. How do you describe a blue you can't hold? Today's sky was that indescribable mix of cobalt and periwinkle, and the clouds looked like freshly spun white cotton candy.

"They said it might rain later," her grandma said. She had both hands on the wheel and sat on a folded red-wool blanket that'd never been anywhere other than her grandparents' car. "And those big clouds usually mean rain." A road map poked out from the sun visor; its faded roads and highways looked like veins. A sticker for an overdue oil change rode next to a parking pass for her grandparents' senior-living complex in the bottom-left corner of the windshield.

"I know. It's just so pretty before it rains," Lexi said. "The clouds are so big and close. It feels like you could touch them."

"I think about that too sometimes." Her grandma kept her eyes on the road. "Mostly when I think about heaven. I imagine sitting on one while I watch all of you. It makes me happy."

"Don't say that." Lexi turned toward her grandma. "That's a horrible thought."

"Why? It's true." Her grandma's smile was small but sweet. Her words were casual and unapologetic. She was simply stating fact.

Lexi was without words. It was another reminder of her grandma's age, maybe the worst yet because it came from her grandma's mouth. She turned back to the window, hoping the tears that'd begun to sting her eyes could hold on long enough not to fall.

"So it's a deal," her grandma said after a few minutes. "Whenever you see those big clouds, think of me looking out for you." She reached for Lexi's hand and gave it a squeeze. "Because whether I'm here or there, you're not getting rid of me."

"OK, Grandma." Lexi returned the squeeze and looked to meet her grandma's eyes, her tears right on the edge. "It's a deal. I love you," she said and turned back to the window before her grandma could see them fall.

Her grandma smiled again. "But I love you most," she said.

CHAPTER 15

ALWAYS

Lexi kept sifting her weight in the canoe. Canoes were hard enough to sit in, but sitting behind her crush left her particularly unstable.

"Ahh!" she shrieked. The shock of the water caught her breath. It was cold and hit without warning. She heard Justin laugh as she wiped her face.

"Oh, sorry; did I get you?" he asked sarcastically without turning to see the damage.

Lexi returned fire, but he was ready and dodged the wave. She tried again but only succeeded in dropping her paddle and rocking the boat. Their laughter overtook Lexi's annoyance as they continued across the lake.

It was beautiful. The canoe's image was mirrored in the water; only their rowing caused distortion. The clouds she'd watched with her grandma only an hour before whipped across the sky. A darkness rode their coattails erasing her favorite blue. The smells of wet dust and damp pine overtook the coconut in her sunscreen, and she could hear thunder rolling in the distance; rain was coming.

Justin removed his sunglasses and looked over his shoulder. With a wink, he asked, "What do you say—shall we hike Flagpole?"

"Definitely!" Lexi answered. "I mean, is there really a better time to hike a mountain than during a lightning storm?"

"Can't think of a single one." He smiled and turned back to face forward. They were more than halfway to Angela's and Garrett's. "This is perfect," he continued. "We can grab Angela and Garrett and head up. It will be just like last time."

"So a total success," Lexi said jokingly.

"Then again"—he looked over his shoulder once more—"a competitive game of Uno and s'mores sound pretty awesome too."

"I vote Uno and chocolate," Lexi said without hesitation.

"All right," Justin said. "Uno it is."

The damp air was still. Usually, they'd have to dodge the chalet taxi, fishing lines, and familiar faces headed to cabins, but the dark sky and certainty of rain left them alone on the lake. Their light banter faded into the stillness as they enjoyed the uncharacteristic quiet.

"Thanks for listening to me." Justin paid her the softly spoken compliment without looking back. His delivery was familiar, and as much as she craved serious moments with him, she couldn't help her uncomfortableness when Justin talked to her as a peer. The moments usually caught her off guard and were seemingly thrown out as afterthoughts and always when they were alone.

"About what?" she asked hoping to pull more from him.

"The whole college thing, Natalie, whatever. I appreciate it. I feel like you get me."

His nonchalance fed her doubts on everything she was hoping for and all she'd begun to speculate. She couldn't imagine that he'd be this casual with someone he liked, so she suggested the obvious. "Well," she said, "I've known you forever, so…"

"No," he said, cutting her off. "I mean, I know, but it's not like a family thing. I tell you things I wouldn't tell my family. There's something about you; you make it easy."

His confession melted her in the middle, and as the warmth radiated, she knew her cheeks would turn pink with the heat.

"No problem. Anytime," she said. But what she'd wanted to say was always. He could talk to her always. Saying anytime felt inadequate; it was too every day. Always was worth more, always had meaning, but it also brought complication, because always is a promise. So instead, she kept it easy, like he said. "You're going to be awesome in college, and for what it's worth, I think you're better off without Natalie." Then in a surprising burst of confidence, she blurted, "She wasn't right for you."

For a moment, the quiet was back. Lexi looked at her feet and inwardly cursed herself before Justin turned in his seat to face her. "So who is?" he asked. Lexi looked up and caught his soft smile. And for a second, she returned it leaving his question to hang in the air. All Lexi had to do was reach for it, but she didn't. It was too heavy for her to hold; it was too much weight—it was too real an opportunity. She wasn't ready to let go of the fantasy; it felt too good. In her fantasies, Justin was hers. Doubt, heartbreak—neither fit into her daydreams. If she answered his question honestly, she'd have to deal with reality, and she wasn't ready to take the chance.

"Hey, guys!" Angela called through cupped hands. Angela's call gave Lexi somewhere to duck, a place to hide, a chance to exit what was quickly becoming an awkward conversation.

"Hi!" Lexi called back making quick use of the paddle she'd forgotten about until that moment. Justin followed Lexi's lead and helped paddle them to the dock. Angela didn't have to be Lexi's best friend to sense Lexi's uncomfortableness. Justin hopped out of the canoe and headed toward Garrett who stood on the deck above. Angela reached for Lexi and helped pull her onto the dock.

Lexi gripped Angela's hand and widened her eyes at her, hoping her look could say everything she couldn't. She didn't want to risk Justin hearing her. She needed to get Angela alone. Angela returned the look and gave a nod that brought Lexi relief.

Garrett, Justin, and a few of the friends Lexi had met while playing washers were also there. She waved and managed a hi, before

Angela pulled her into the kitchen with the excuse of tracking down the essentials for s'mores. With everyone else outside, they could talk. "Oh my God!" Lexi grabbed Angela by her shoulders and shook her. "This is crazy!" She dropped her hands and turned away from Angela. "I think I'm going to throw up."

"Wait! Hang on." It was Angela's turn to grab Lexi by the shoulders. She spun her round to face her. "Take a deep breath." Lexi looked at Angela and inhaled deeply. "Where's Natalie?"

"She's gone. He broke up with her." Lexi continued to breathe heavily.

"Why?" Angela questioned. Her eyes rolled trying to make sense of all Lexi was saying. "When did he do that?"

"This morning or last night. Whatever. She left this morning. He said he didn't think she understood him."

"Seriously? No way! This is awesome!" Angela was genuinely excited. "When are you guys going to hook up?"

"Angela! Shhh," Lexi begged. "We're not. Stop it."

"Well, why not? You guys would be so cute together. The perfect lake couple. You could even get married here. Remember, last year, Hannah and Sam? How awesome was their wedding? Of course, I'll be in it and…"

"Angela! Seriously. Stop."

"Sorry. You know I'm kidding. Honestly, though, in my humble opinion, this isn't all in your head. There's something there. There's always been something there."

There it was again, that word "always." The word she clung to. She desperately wanted it to be always, and she wanted to believe Angela.

"What's up in there?" Garrett called from the front door. "I thought you guys were getting stuff for s'mores?"

"One second," Angela called back. "Look, the dance is tomorrow; maybe that's the opportunity you guys need. I'll drive us to the dance. There's a lot of people coming from this side of the lake. If we take our big boat, we can fit eight of us, and I'll make sure you guys share a seat."

The rest of the afternoon was a haze filled with lost card games and burned marshmallows. Lost in her thoughts, Lexi saw the first drops of rain on the single paned window. She started to count them, something she'd always done on long car rides when hours seemed longer. Soon she lost count. The rain came too fast, and the drops were too fat. They slid into each other creating puddles that ran into larger pools.

The crack overhead seemed loud enough to pierce the roof. The storm wanted inside. One more boom might do it. A light flooded the room as the storm landed above. When it was over, all that remained were sticky patches of melted marshmallow on the coffee table and empty soda cans. The storm had also left Lexi's stomach. Her nausea was gone, and the break from both was the chance Lexi and Justin needed to paddle back.

In the canoe and almost home, Justin broke the silence. "So the dance?" he questioned. Lexi's heart skipped briefly but stopped with his follow-up, "How are we getting there?"

"Oh…" She deflated. "Angela said she could take us."

"Awesome. I've got my bow tie and Hawaiian shirt ready to go."

The memory of the shirt cracked a smile on Lexi's lips. "Fantastic," she said.

At the dock, Justin reached for Lexi's hand to help pull her from the canoe. "So I have to ask." His eyes twinkled. "Are you excited?"

Lexi smiled. He hadn't let go of her hand. "Always, Justin. Always."

CHAPTER 16

SOMETHING TANGIBLE

Lexi's reflection smiled at her. She wished for her bathroom mirror at home, but the medicine cabinet in the bathroom was as good as she'd get. For the second time, she dumped her toiletry bag into the sink. Nude eye shadows dusted the porcelain with soft pinks and muted browns, while her eyeliner and favorite pink-and-green tube of mascara circled to a stop on the drain. It was the first time she'd done her makeup at the lake, and she wasn't used to the limited counter space. If only she could find her cherry lip gloss, she'd be ready. Even with limited lake amenities, she'd managed to pull it off. Just like most of her lake clothes, her dress for prom was secondhand courtesy of her best friend's sister. She remembered when Brooke wore it to homecoming and how jealous she was that she'd have to wait two years before she'd get to go. The dress had capped selves and was short without feeling a need to pull on it. Most importantly, it looked cute with her Converse.

Another look in the mirror, she grimaced. She hated how one side of her hair flipped under and the other out; while the inevitable boat ride allowed her the excuse for letting it go, it didn't stop her from messing with it. Why can't I get it to look right? she thought. She had so much riding on things working out perfectly.

More hairspray, then a quick glance at the bathroom clock. Angela promised to pick them up no later than 6:00 p.m.; her time was up.

"What do you think?" Lexi stepped up out of the bathroom and into the kitchen. Haley danced past as Lexi's mom and dad were starting dinner. Her aunt and uncle were taking the evening off and visiting friends across the lake.

"I think you look beautiful," Haley said as she reached up to touch Lexi's dress. The dress pulled Haley's hands like a magnet; it was rare to see anyone in something other than a T-shirt.

"You look nice, sweetheart." Her dad always made it a point to tell her how beautiful she was. It didn't matter that it was prom; he said the same thing every morning before school, yet it never felt inauthentic. "Have fun tonight," he said.

Her mom turned away from the stove; her eyes scanned Lexi top to bottom. "But those shoes..." She couldn't help herself. Her mom had a habit of making her feel self-conscious with the smallest of comments.

"Mom, everyone will be in tennis shoes; it's the lake. It's these or flip-flops."

"Then I vote flip-flops," her mom said. "You're in such a cute dress. At least the flip-flops will look less bulky. You can't wear a summer dress with tennis shoes."

"Fine." Annoyed that her mom had a valid point she left the kitchen and walked into the main room in search of her sandals. Her grandma was seated below the window.

"They're right there by the door," she said. Of course her grandma knew what she needed; the size of the cabin made kitchen conversations into cabin conversations. "You look gorgeous, honey." With some effort her grandma stood to hold Lexi's cheeks in her hands.

"Thanks, Grandma," Lexi said.

Her grandma cupped Lexi's cheeks and brought her close. "I love you," she said as their foreheads met.

"I love you too, Grandma." The sound of Angela and Garrett's boat flipped Lexi's stomach. "OK, I've gotta go! Angela is here." She grabbed her bag, double-checking for her travel hairbrush and lip gloss. She thought about taking a sweater but didn't want to carry it, and the sun had been hot enough during the day that she assumed the night would hold the heat.

"Don't wait up!" She threw the advice over her shoulder as she stepped out the door and onto the deck. She made it in time to catch Justin leaving his cabin. Like last year, he wore a fitted black suit and his grandpa's famous Hawaiian shirt and bow tie.

"Look at you, all grown up," he called as he walked to meet Lexi as she headed down. Lexi smiled at the compliment and felt compelled to spin around to give the full effect.

"And look at you…" She made it a point to take a good, long look at him. "You're still working on it." The ease in their teasing distracted her anxiety. See how easy things could be, she thought. Why was she so nervous?

"Guys! Let's go!" Angela's plea broke the spell, and Lexi's anxiety flooded back. The boat was full with kids from their side of the lake, but Angela had kept her promise. She'd successfully arranged the seating, and the only place for Justin and Lexi to sit was next to each other.

The ride to the chalet was fast, and the wind made it hard to hear anything but the motor. Once they arrived, they were greeted by Joe and Doug. Joe and Doug had cabins on the same shore as Lexi's and Justin's families, but it'd been a few summers since she'd seen them. The boys motioned for the group to follow them around back. Out of sight, Doug pulled a flask from his pocket.

"Cool, right?" Doug held it high for everyone to see. "I found it in our cabin, in the cupboard with the hard alcohol. It must have been my grandpa's." Every cabin had a cupboard with hard alcohol, leftover from when days ended with a nightcap. Lexi's grandma still enjoyed a sip of scotch every night. Doug's excitement reminded Lexi of a kid in her second-grade class who'd shared his grandpa's war medal during show-and-tell. "You guys want some?" Doug asked with high hopes.

"What is it?" Garrett asked. Lexi remembered feeling sorry for the boy in her class; he was so excited to show off the medal, but he couldn't compete with the kid who'd brought in a Luke Skywalker action figure. No one cared about his grandpa's prized possession.

Doug threw his head back and took a swig. "Whiskey." He choked. "It was this, tequila, or vodka. A pick your poison kind of thing."

"Nope. It's all yours," Garrett said as he turned to head into the dance.

"Justin?" Doug pushed the flask on him.

"No, thanks, I'm good." Justin took after Garrett, and Lexi and the rest of the group from the boat followed. Everyone passed except Lexi, who didn't answer; somehow, she didn't feel like the question applied to her. Only Joe accepted Doug's offer. Lexi watched over her shoulder as Joe took a sip and then coughed repeatedly in an effort to keep it down. Just the smell of alcohol worried her. Her friends didn't drink, but she'd kept watch at the bathroom door while her cousin puked her guts out at her uncle's fiftieth birthday. After that, Lexi swore she'd never be that girl. She hoped Joe and Doug would avoid the same fate.

Inside the chalet, strings of Christmas lights cast a glow across a cleared dance floor. The pockets of dark hid racks of Summit Lake T-shirts and postcards and stacks of water bottles. Someone had set up a sheet with the words "Summit Lake Prom" spray-painted across it. Paper streamers framed the sheet, and a camera atop a tripod focused on it, creating a make-shift photo booth. On the floor a box of beat-up hats, boas, and old sunglasses waited to be worn.

"We definitely have to get a picture of all of us." Angela pointed.

Garrett was in agreement. "I call the sailor's hat."

The cash-register counter provided a space for drinks and snacks. An iPod played a playlist curated from a clipboard that'd hung in the chalet for the past few days collecting song requests. Lexi hoped her pick made the cut. In her mind, her song would begin, and within seconds Justin would ask her to dance. They'd sway slowly; he'd tuck a strand of hair behind her ear, look deep into her eyes, and lean in giving her the kiss. She'd daydreamed of for so long that a small piece of her believed it was a memory and not a dream.

Within minutes, Angela grabbed her hand, and they ran into the center of the room. Lexi loved to dance, and as fast song after fast song played, she and Angela drifted further into their own world. On the few occasions, a slow song came on, and they left the floor in search of water. Food wasn't as important; it was hard to get excited about a bowl of crushed Doritos. Then another "favorite" song of theirs would play, and they'd hurry back onto the floor. She wasn't reminded of Justin until she heard it, the first few notes to her song, the song that'd she'd hoped would change her life forever. She scanned the room for Justin and spotted him approaching Angela, but before she could move, Garrett reached out a hand and asked her to dance.

"I have to say you're looking lovely tonight, Lexi Sterling." Garrett had caught her off guard, and she felt her cheeks warm at his surprisingly sweet words. "But let's not get ahead of ourselves," he warned. "This is a compliment coming from someone who thinks of you as a sister."

He spun her slowly and greeted her return to front with a sly smile. "I know you like him." Lexi felt the flush of her cheeks grow hotter. Her mind swam, and she began to drown in fear. How much did Garrett know? Had he said anything to Justin? "He's a good guy," he continued with a softened smile. "Lucky too. If a girl is going to have a crush on you, you're the kind of girl guys hope for." Her anxieties had caused Lexi to miss the compliment; she hadn't heard anything past, "I know you like him."

"Please tell me you didn't tell him anything," she said.

"He already knows." He shrugged. "You're not the best at hiding your feelings. I've always admired that about you. When you talk, you give people a piece of you." Garrett's words threw her. It wasn't like him to say more than what was needed. Why was he telling her this? She had so many questions. "I think that's what he likes about you. You're not jaded." He paused. "I guess…you've got an innocence to you."

Oh, that word "innocent," she couldn't escape it. It seemed to follow her around like the annoying little sister she didn't have. "Innocent" was a word used to describe a child, and she was tired of people thinking of her that way. She hated it as much as people describing her as cute, which always seemed to be followed up with a pat on her head.

"Wait!" The flood of information was just sorting itself out. "Did you say he likes me?"

"He hasn't said anything to me, nothing concrete, anyway, but yeah, I think he does." The song ended, and Garrett thanked her for the dance before they headed for Angela and Justin.

Lexi's head was spinning when Justin grabbed her, "Hey, I was just going to get you." Justin seemed rushed. "I think I need to take Joe home." He looked around to see if anyone was watching. "The whiskey was more than he could handle."

"OK." Lexi hadn't had time to process anything; her mind was stuck in her conversation with Garrett. Like telling someone thank you when they ask you how you're doing.

"I'm going to drive him home in his boat, and then he can grab it from our dock in the morning."

Once her mind caught up, it immediately registered that someone was in need, and Lexi jumped. "Let me help," she offered. She'd said the words a million times; it was a habit of hers to take on a motherly roll. It was something she did without thought. If someone needed help, she'd be there.

"No, it's OK; I've got him," Justin reassured her. "You stay and enjoy the dance. You can head home with everyone else."

"No, I think she's right." Angela managed to wink at Lexi unnoticed. "She's awesome in situations like these. Plus, it's almost over, and if you go together, we won't have to make a second stop. Garrett and I can go straight to our dock." Lexi had offered help without alternative motives, but she loved where Angela was going. Throw-up hadn't been part of her fantasy, but time alone with Justin was.

Together, Lexi and Justin managed to get Joe into his boat. He was a happy drunk and slurred thank-yous repeatedly. He almost made it home before puking. Thankfully, he leaned far enough over the side to avoid getting anything in the boat. After working for what seemed like an hour, Lexi and Justin managed to get him up the hill and onto an outdoor cot on his cabin's back deck. The hope was he'd sleep it off, before having to face his family in the morning.

"Well...that was..." Justin was at a loss for words.

"All part of the fun," Lexi suggested.

"What? Where are you going with this, Lexi? Fun?"

"That's what my grandma always says when something goes wrong, 'It's all part of the fun.'"

Back in Joe's boat, it was only a five-minute ride to Lexi and Justin's dock. Stepping onto their dock, Lexi looked to the stars for a reason to stall. She never understood how the sky at Summit could be the same as the lackluster dots that hovered in the sky at home. At the lake the sky was filled with stars, almost as though they were poured into the sky like sand.

"They're incredible, right?" Justin had followed Lexi's gaze. "I can't believe how many there are. It almost seems fake."

"It's so different from the sky I see at home." Lexi's eyes stayed focused on the stars; she hoped it'd prolong the inevitable goodnight. The carefully planned expectations for the evening had slipped away quietly. Between dancing with Angela, unexpected insight from Garrett, and the smell of puke, she'd lost the butterflies. All she wanted now was a little more time.

"Hey, there's Cassiopeia." Justin pointed at the familiar constellation. "I always remember it because it looks like a *W*. Somehow it's supposed to look like a queen sitting on her throne, but I could never make it out."

Lexi dropped her head to the lights across the lake. "I like to see the lights on in the cabins." With the official start of Summit Lake Day tomorrow, the shores of the lake had come alive that afternoon. Between the busy hum of motors, the air had filled with screams from delighted water-skiers, echoing laughter, the barks of happy dogs running the banks, and yelled welcomes to friends and family. But the dark brought quiet, and the only reminder that the cabins were full of the best parts of summer were the lights. "It means people are here. That everyone is here."

They were about halfway to their doors when Lexi stopped to sit. The air was cool, but the granite was warm on the backs of her legs. If only she could hit pause. Finally, a piece of her night was fitting in, and she wanted to soak it up.

Justin stood behind her. She could feel him wanting to leave. She couldn't blame him. She took a chance and kept up the conversation. "The first time I saw a shooting star was here."

"Me too." He yawned. "Did you make a wish?"

"I think I forgot to." Lexi searched her mind. "I was so excited to see it." The details of the memory were clouded. She'd seen countless shooting stars since and hadn't thought back to the first in years, but the memory of her most recent wish on a shooting star was vivid. She'd wished for Justin to kiss her. She breathed in the cooling mountain air; it felt good on her face. Along with the dust and pine, she smelled just a hint of Justin's cologne, but it was enough to tighten her heart. Minutes passed in silence before Justin spoke.

"OK, I think I'm going to head in." Lexi closed her eyes in disappointment. Whatever moment she'd hoped for had passed. "After all, it's a big day tomorrow," he said. "I have to kick your butt in the scavenger hunt."

Lexi laughed. The scavenger hunt was an event for kids under six, something for them to do while the older kids and adults participated in more complex events. "It's a pretty competitive event," Lexi joked. "The six-year-olds are ruthless."

"I heard a four-year-old bit a kid last year." Lexi turned in time to see Justin's eyes twinkle. "Something about who saw the stick first," he said.

She laughed again. "I heard about that." She paused another moment hoping to catch him but knew Justin was too far away for her to grab. In the end, she decided if she couldn't keep him close, she'd hang on to the night. "I think I'm going to stay here for a bit."

"You sure?" he questioned.

"I'm sure. You go on." She didn't bother to watch him. Instead she focused on the moon; by this time of night, it'd climbed high enough to peek out from the tops of the pines. It wasn't full, but it still showed a spotlight on the water. The cool breeze that'd been appreciated only minutes before was steadily growing colder. She promised herself only a few more minutes before she'd head inside. Just then, she was surprised with a jacket draped around her shoulders.

"Thought you might get cold," he said. "I couldn't let you sit out here without a jacket." Justin had come back. His jacket felt and smelled like heaven and warmed her insides.

"Thanks," she said as Justin turned to head back. Her hand had briefly touched his as he'd wrapped the jacket around her, but her touch hadn't been enough to make him stay. She pulled the dark-gray cotton hoodie tighter before slipping her arms inside. The sleeves hung past her hands, and the sides wrapped around her like her favorite bathrobe. There was no point in zipping it.

The cabin was dark by the time she came in. She didn't bother to brush her teeth before climbing into the loft. Her knee hit the edge of the chimney, and she had a brief flash of how much easier the climb had been as a kid. She knew there'd be a bruise in the morning. She felt for her pajamas and managed to find them without her flashlight. Before lying down, she slipped back into Justin's jacket. Memories of the night flooded her. The most repetitive being what Garrett said. She couldn't help but keep going back to it; he'd said that he thought Justin liked her. With Justin's jacket wrapped around her and the possibility that he felt the same as she did heavy in her mind, she fell into a deep sleep. She didn't need to dream; she had a real piece of him to hold on to.

CHAPTER 17

THE STARTING LINE

Lexi stood at the kitchen sink; she was waiting for the water on the stove to boil. Her eyes were drawn like magnets to an imperfection of a thin crack that ran across the bottom of the windowpane. She'd never known the window without a crack, and it was always the first place her eyes fell. Her mind would see the crack and then drift into thought as though it was the starting line for her daydreams. If asked she wouldn't have known what the view from the window was, only that there was a crack she couldn't see past.

The slow whistle of the kettle brought her out of the fog of her thoughts. She readjusted Justin's sweatshirt to sit higher on her shoulders; the morning was cooler than it had been. She reached for a jar above the stove that contained a collection of tea bags and instant coffee and was happy to find a hot-chocolate packet hidden among them. Next she opened the cupboard that housed a mismatched set of coffee mugs. The absence of her grandma's mug left a vacancy on the otherwise-crowded shelf. She couldn't remember the last time she'd beat her grandma to the kettle. Even those mornings when the heat of the loft pushed her awake sooner then she'd like, her grandma would already be on her second cup of coffee. She joked that it was her job to get the sun up. She never teased Lexi for sleeping in, and Lexi wondered if she might be a bit jealous of her ability to sleep late into the morning.

Today was different, though. Lexi had set an alarm on her phone, the first time she'd turned it on since arriving; it was the morning of Summit Lake Day, and she wanted to make sure she was up in time to help make sandwiches, pack the cooler, and gather the beach chairs and towels. She'd also have to help get the boats up to the Scout camp. Most of her family would ride in their small aluminum boat, but Lexi and her dad would follow behind in the canoe and kayak.

Her plan was to meet Angela there. Thankfully, Angela had asked to have Summit Lake Day off her first morning on the job in early June. Labor Day weekend was one of the busiest at the chalet, and they needed as many people as possible to staff the store, drive the taxi boats, and run the boat dock. Angela also asked for Garrett, and they both managed to get out of work. Lexi was looking forward to winning first place with Angela in the Clothes Exchange, and Garrett and Justin had agreed to partner in the log roll; this was the first year they were old enough to participate. The log roll was the highlight of the games. A giant log was pushed into shoulder high water, while one person stood at each end to steady it. Then two teams of two climbed on top. On the count of three, the spotters would let go, and the team with a member who stayed on the longest moved to the next round. Eventually, it got down to two people, sometimes partner against partner, and then there'd be a final round. The winner received a wrestler's belt with "Log Roll Champion" burned into the leather. The belt returned each year and was passed to the new champion.

"Where's your shirt?" Her dad gently nudged Lexi from behind and worked to slip past her. It was a tight squeeze in the kitchen, between the large kitchen table, stove, and 1950s propane refrigerator that regularly froze over but took days to freeze ice cubes.

Lexi saw that her dad was already dressed in his "Team Sterling" shirt. "Mind if I steal a little of your water?" he asked.

Lexi grabbed the kettle. "Don't worry, Dad," she said and poured some of the boiling water into his outstretched mug. "I'll make sure I put it on before we go."

Grabbing a spoon from the drawer, Lexi headed to the front room just missing Haley bouncing out of the bathroom in her pale-pink "Team Sterling" shirt. Haley's shirt looked more like a dress than a T-shirt, and Lexi bent to tie one side of it into a knot. "No, I like it this way." Haley pushed her off. Lexi's aunt followed Haley out of the bathroom and caught Lexi's kind gesture. Her aunt smiled and mouthed the words "thank you" before she chased Haley with a hairbrush and bottle of sunscreen.

Wanting to escape her cousin's squeals, Lexi continued to the porch. Seeing the dock, she was reminded that she wore Justin's sweatshirt and briefly panicked that she'd be caught with it on. It was one thing to borrow it for warmth; it was another to continue wearing it as if it was hers. But the dock was empty of Robertses' boats. As much as she longed to keep Justin's jacket, her compulsion to return it was greater. She worried that the longer she held on to it, the more obvious her feelings for him would be. There was no doubt that Justin was aware of the crush she had on him; she'd lost that battle, but maybe there was a chance she could cover how big of a crush. If he really knew how she felt, she was sure she'd scare him off.

Finished with her hot chocolate, she went inside to get ready. In the loft, she took off Justin's sweatshirt and folded it neatly on her sleeping bag while daydreaming about the conversation she could have with him when she gave it back. She couldn't wait to tell Angela that he'd given her his sweatshirt.

A moment later, with her hair pulled back as much as short hair allowed, a pair of shorts on, and her light-blue "Team Sterling" shirt covering her bathing suit, she walked back to the kitchen.

There she grabbed one end of the packed cooler, while her mom held the other, and they headed for the dock. Looking across the lake, it seemed that the sprinkling of lights that'd lit the cabins the night before had magically transformed into boats. There were dozens more than there had been all summer. The lake was criss-crossed with wakes as everyone headed toward the channel. A few more trips back and forth and Lex had helped her grandma, mom, aunt, uncle, and Haley settle into the boat with all their gear. Her dad was already pushing off in the kayak and she was about to follow him in the canoe when she heard Justin yell her name.

He stood on his porch with his hands cupped to his mouth. "Can I grab a ride?" His face was shaded by his familiar baseball hat, and he wore swim trunks with his faded Summit shirt. Lexi's stomach defied gravity and somersaulted into her throat. She closed her eyes and took a breath to steady herself. For the first time, she questioned how it was that she continually looked forward to this feeling of nausea. "My grandparents are already there setting up, and my parents are catching a ride with the Elliots, but that's not for another twenty minutes," he called down. "I promised my grandpa I'd head up as soon as I could. He wants help setting up the dock."

The Scout camp was empty of manmade structures. It'd been cleared of everything years before when the camp closed. A temporary dock was brought out and put together every year for Summit Lake Day. It provided a stage for the announcer and a starting line for the races. Most everyone on the lake had a volunteer position for the day's games or the night's bonfire. Whether it was announcing, making prizes, lifeguarding, baking, organizing songbooks like Nancy, or hauling firewood, everyone helped. Without the whole of the lake, there wouldn't be a competition. Lexi usually helped with the kid's scavenger hunt, and she assumed it'd be the same this year. She looked from Justin back to her dad waiting in the kayak. He was waiting for her.

"What do you say?" Justin's shadow blocked the shimmer of sun on the water. He'd walked to the canoe and was waiting for her reply. Of course he could ride with her and her dad. He'd done it plenty of times; that's how they'd grown up. If someone needed a ride, a spotter for water-skiing, or wanted to fish, everyone was welcome on a boat. But with all that'd been happening, the little moments she was sure they'd shared, things felt different. Things were different, and she didn't want her dad paddling alongside. She was tongue-tied. Everything felt weird and complicated. She wanted Justin in her boat, but not if her dad was going to follow.

Before she could find the words, her dad called out, "Hey, Lexi, I'll see you there." She watched as her dad gave a wave, smiled, and headed for the channel. A brief feeling of guilt trickled into her stomach, but it wasn't enough to dampen her excitement. He was doing what she'd wanted; he was giving her space. He was treating her like a grown up.

She faced Justin. "Totally," she said. "Hop in."

"Thanks," he said. "I appreciate it."

They pushed off the dock, and Lexi handed Justin a paddle. Their ride was far from what Lexi had hoped. They were regularly interrupted by people shouting hellos and enthusiastic shouts of promises to beat them in their competitions. Justin asked her about the events she planned to compete in and if she and Angela were shooting for first in the Clothes Exchange. He reminded her that he and Garrett were attempting the log roll and made her promise not to laugh when they failed. As they got closer, they scanned the shore for a place to tie up. Just like every year, a large number of different sized boats outlined the limited shoreline. Eventually, they squeezed between two kayaks and found a downed tree perfect for an anchor.

"Thanks for the ride," Justin said without waiting to help Lexi. "I'm going to go find Garrett." He waded in the ankle-deep water and started for the trail. "Oh!" he said as if he'd forgotten the most important thing. "You better cheer for us when the time comes."

"That goes both ways," Lexi reminded.

"Of course." He winked.

The ground was damp from the night before, and Lexi was thankful to see her dad had managed to secure seating with the placement of a tarp. They'd gotten smarter in the last few years, bringing a tarp instead of towels. The towels always ended up black with mud and heavy with water; there were too many people running back and forth from the lake to keep towels dry.

The first event was the kids' six-and-under swim, and Lexi was in time to see Haley at the start dock. The announcer blew the whistle. "Go, Haley!" she screamed. She watched her cousin hesitate before launching herself into the clear water. The cheers from the crowd grew as the group gained momentum toward the finish. With only a stroke behind first, Haley took second.

"Looks like Team Sterling is off to a good start." Angela snuck up from behind and playfully bumped shoulders with Lexi. She reached to exam Haley's award and smiled as Haley showed off proudly. "Awesome job, Haley! That's going to look great on your cabin wall." But Haley had already forgotten that Angela was talking to her and ran off to show others her big win. "Good news!" Angela flipped her attention to Lexi. "Garrett's going to let us use his shirt for the race!" Angela held up a large white shirt with thin fabric. "And it's perfect, because we can get into it easily, and it won't be super heavy."

"This is great." Lexi felt the fabric and saw that the material was almost see through. "We've totally got it this year." The idea of winning had momentarily replaced any thoughts of Justin and her news about his jacket.

"Wait! More importantly." Angela couldn't believe she'd forgotten about the night before. "I haven't asked you about Justin. Did anything happen after you guys took Joe home?"

"He gave me his jacket!" Lexi smiled, happy that she had something to share.

"And…" Angela held her breath.

"That's it. We dropped Joe off and then headed home. We stopped for a second to look at the stars, and I said I wanted to stay longer, hoping he'd stay, but he went inside. Then a few minutes later he came back and wrapped his sweatshirt around me."

Angela let out a sigh of frustration. "Lexi, it's so obvious he likes you." She couldn't believe there wasn't more. "He ditched Natalie, he talks to you about stuff guys never talk about, and…I'm not supposed to tell you this, but…he told Garrett he likes you!"

"What?" Lexi was taken aback. She thought back to her conversation with Garrett at prom. Maybe he knew more than he'd led on. He'd seemed so nonchalant. "When?" She had so many questions. "How do you know?"

"Garrett told me at the dance, after you and Justin left."

"Hang on…" Lexi's mind was spinning. "But what'd Justin say?" She needed more information. She wanted to know how Justin said it. Was he serious? Or did he say it to shut Garrett up? What did he mean by he likes me? Does he want to date me? Kiss me? What if Garrett just wanted to mess with me, so he told Angela that Justin liked me, because he knew Angela would say something to me? This news was huge, and Angela was disappointingly light on details.

"I don't know." She shrugged. "He didn't give me a play by play. I don't think they had a huge heart to heart over it. They're guys. My guess is that Garrett just called him out, and then they dropped it. Justin's not an idiot; it's not like you guys were going to start dating. But, Lexi, you better do something soon because he's leaving on Sunday."

Lexi knew Angela was right, but it hurt to hear that Garrett and Justin could drop it that easily. She wasn't stupid either. She knew they weren't destined for a relationship, but knowing even the possibility was out of the question crushed her.

"He's leaving? Why?" Lexi thought she had one more week with Justin.

"I think his mom has to go back to work, and he's got water-polo practice."

"This sucks. What am I going to do?"

"We'll think of something, but I think we're only one event away from the Clothes Exchange. Come on; let's get ready."

Lexi pushed her disappointment and worry deep into her stomach. She need to focus on the event. This was their year to win. The plan was to have Angela start since she was the slower swimmer. She'd race to Lexi wearing the shirt and flip it over Lexi's head, and then Lexi could use her speed to make up for any lost time.

The whistle blew, and Lexi watched as Angela surprisingly crept into first. Reaching Lexi, only a few strokes behind the lead, she pulled the back of the shirt over Lexi's head. Lexi pushed her arms through the armholes at the same time she took her first stroke. Lexi didn't open her eyes underwater but took a quick look with each breath. It was going to be close. She only needed a few more strokes; she put her head down and kicked as hard as she could. Her hand hit the dock with a bang, and she shot up before her head did the same. They'd done it. First place was theirs.

Only a few minutes into their celebration, a whistle blew, signaling for log-roll participants to make their way to the lake.

It was almost too close to tell, but in the end Garrett and Justin lost the chance to move forward. The final was between the long-time champion Jorden Redding and Miles Moore who wore his traditional American flag swim trunks. Everyone cheered for Miles, but in the end, Jorden got to keep his belt.

The afternoon had reached its high, and people were thinking more about dinner than what they had for lunch. Lexi sat cross-legged with Haley wrapped in a towel in her lap. People joked the year before that Haley had won the lap-sitting contest, because most of her time had been spent snuggled in laps instead of participating in the competitions. She hugged Haley tight. She'd lost sight of Justin after his loss in the log roll, and Angela had already headed home. She let the sounds of laughter, shouts of encouragement, and exaggerated cries of disappointment wash over her. Boats lapped at the shore, and the lines between families and friends blurred. This was the magic of the lake; there was nothing else like it, and she felt incredibly lucky to have it.

Lexi's aunt helped Haley up from Lexi's lap. "We're going to head back. Do you want to come with us? We're going to pull the kayak. We could tie the canoe on and pull that too."

"No, it's OK. I've got it." Lexi had hopes that Justin was lingering and would need a ride back.

She waved good-bye to her family and pulled her legs to her chest; her toes were inches from the water, and she watched fallen pine needles dodge the wakes that pushed them toward shore. She was scanning the crowd for Justin when a warm touch turned her attention. Her stomach spun on instinct; it was him. "Hey, I'm going to catch a ride back with my family," he said. "I'll see you at the bonfire?" His question paused the disappointment that'd immediately started to fill her.

She looked at him. "I'll be there." She managed a smile. His eyes locked with hers, and his smile said everything Lexi wanted him to say aloud. She hoped her smile said as much. "I'll definitely be there."

CHAPTER 18

SMOKE AND FIRE

Captured by the cramped quarters, the smell of lavender swirled in the shower steam. Although good for the environment and the cabin's almost original plumbing, the earth-friendly natural shampoo and conditioner did nothing to help Lexi's hair but clean it. She wiped the mirror and stared at the girl who was looking back. She had so many questions for her. Mainly, what did she plan to do about Justin? This was the last night she'd have with him, and she had no idea how it was going to end. A year of daydreams leading to these final weeks of summer and how different it was supposed to be from all the others. And in the end, she felt no closer to Justin than when she'd started. She'd seen hints of things, maybe a possibility, but she was done with the fantasy; she wanted him. She wanted to leave Summit with a memory that was more than a missed chance. She wanted her first kiss; she wanted Justin to be her first kiss. She caught a smile from the girl in the mirror; just the thought of Justin kissing her made it hard to breathe. She could feel her heartbeat in her palms.

Justin was leaving tomorrow, and an entire year would separate them before they'd see each other again. Her daydreams were losing their footing; it was hard to be positive when time was limited.

She wandered back through her mind to every missed opportunity and questioned why she hadn't done more to get his attention. She couldn't shake what Angela had said only hours before. Did he really like her? She thought so; he'd shown interest, but could he actually like her for real? Did he see her as a cute girl with a summer crush or as something more? She wasn't anything like Natalie; she was some soon to be freshman, a childhood friend he grew up playing card games with. At most, she was someone to flirt with. She couldn't believe he'd see her as anything more. Right? The girl in the mirror didn't answer.

At the bottom of her duffel bag, she found the clean pair of jeans and long-sleeved shirt she'd saved for tonight. She'd brought a beanie but didn't like how it covered her hair. Before she'd got it cut, her hair hung past her shoulders, but now she looked bald with it on. She pulled it off and brushed her hair again. The girl in the mirror watched without opinion, but something about her caught Lexi's attention, and she stopped to stare. There was something different, something in her eyes. She saw the experiences she had over the last three weeks reflected back. She thought about how she'd become more aware of her grandma's age, how different sailing with her dad had been, Justin confiding in her about Natalie and college, and how she helped Justin bring Joe home after prom. But the difference wasn't just her eyes; it was how she carried herself. The last three weeks had changed her, and the more she considered everything, both the big and the small details, she realized she wasn't a little kid anymore. The girl in the mirror gave a knowing nod and smiled. Lexi liked the girl looking back at her and decided if there was a chance to kiss Justin tonight, she was going to take it.

She met her family on the deck. A faded pink had washed over the blue sky of the day's competition and filled the empty spaces around the trees and mountain peaks. The deck felt smaller with everyone on it at once, and she was struck by the sharp contrast between Haley's enthusiastic skipping and her grandma's carefully placed steps. Lexi thought back to when her grandpa was alive; he'd also slowed down in his final years and a knot tied in her throat.

"Here, Dad." Lexi hoped to distract herself from the thought. "Let me take the potato salad." Lexi's dad handed her the familiar plastic-wrapped yellow bowl. It always impressed her that her grandma went the extra mile and garnished the top of the salad with paprika and celery leaves. It seemed so elaborate for such a simple side dish. Then again, it wasn't like her grandma to do anything ordinary.

Lexi's dad and uncle helped guide her grandma down the slope to the boat, while Haley swung between Lexi's mom and her aunt. Their boat was only a few years old, and although used when they bought it, it was almost new compared to their previous one. Their old boat was the same one her aunt had learned to water ski behind, and even then it'd been around for a few years. There was a good amount of debate about what to buy and who should pay when the old boat finally died. In the end, the family decided to split the cost evenly among the siblings, which made Lexi's dad very happy, considering the only time her family could use it was during summer at the lake.

With everyone seated and her uncle driving, Lexi's dad passed around name tags. These took the place of tickets for food. If you came with a name tag, the Millers from the chalet knew you'd paid for the BBQ. Lexi smiled; her dad had added a heart above the *i* in her name. Already in the time it took between leaving their cabin and arriving at the BBQ, hints of purple and slate had shaded the pink that'd been above them and silhouetted their surroundings. For the first time, Lexi understood Justin's dislike of dusk. The newly set sun brought a weight with it, a sadness that draped over the colors of the day muting them. She took a deep breath and reminded herself that no matter what happened, she'd be OK.

The line for dinner was long but friendly. The smell of BBQ had a way of relaxing a crowd into easy conversation. This summer it was the North Shore's turn to host the potluck. The same foods—hamburgers, veggie burgers if you wanted, and potluck sides—were offered each year. There were never enough desserts, and Lexi had learned to head there first if she wanted something sweet for later. Her family was in line behind the Nelsons when Justin and Garrett walked past. They already had their hamburgers and were headed toward a large group of teenagers who'd managed to secure premier seating on a downed tree. She watched with her fingers crossed, hoping there'd be room for her close to Justin when she noticed Angela trailing behind.

"Angela!" Lexi called knowing if anyone could save her a seat it'd be her.

"Lexi!" Angela ran to meet Lexi in line careful to keep her hamburger on her plate. "Hey, I was just going to save you a spot next to Justin. This is your last chance; if anything is going to happen, it's happening tonight."

"Shhhh! Angela! God!" Lexi looked around to see if anyone was listening. Her parents were deep in conversation with the people behind them, and her aunt and uncle were busy with Haley.

"What? No one's paying attention. Besides, I didn't say it that loud. Anyway, get your food and meet us over there. Everyone is here; we're all sitting together. You remember Alex, Dan, and Alison from when you played washers. Even Joe made it out, although I doubt he'll be drinking anything other than water tonight."

"Awesome." Lexi was feeling the excitement of possibility growing in her chest. "Thanks." Then just as quickly, she panicked that Angela would do something to ruin things. "Just, please don't say anything to Justin. Promise me you won't say anything." Lexi was next in line to grab her food and Angela had to step back to give her space.

"OK, fine, I won't say anything. But, Lexi…" Angela's voice faded into a whisper. "He likes you. I promise he likes you, and if you want that kiss you've talked about forever, this is your chance."

"I know. Just, just let me get my food, and I'll come over." Lexi's focus was back on the table of sides.

Angela leaned over Lexi's shoulder to whisper in her ear. "You sure you don't want me to remind him how awesome you are?"

"Angela! Seriously. Stop." Lexi could feel the heat of embarrassment in her cheeks.

"OK. I'm done." Angela turned and headed for the group slowing for a moment to call over her shoulder, "I'll just remind him that this is his last chance to kiss you before he leaves."

"Angela!"

"I'm kidding!" Angela threw her hand up in defeat. "I'll go get us seats. See you in a minute."

Lexi couldn't focus. She looked at the table covered with salads, cornbread, and potatoes and felt sick. Her butterflies had turned to worms, and her stomach was crawling with them. The excitement was gone, replaced by the anxiety of how the night would end. The only thing on her plate when she sat in the spot Angela had saved was a small serving of her grandma's potato salad and even that seemed like too much. She felt like she was drowning, and the confidence she'd left her cabin with had already gone under. She was going to throw up.

"Lexi! How goes it?" Justin's one-dimpled smile did little to ease her panic. Everything about this moment felt awkward, even the seemingly normalcy of it. "Not hungry?"

"Umm, not really," Lexi said.

"Well, if you change your mind, I managed to steal this." Justin held out his hand and showed her a brownie wrapped in a napkin.

"It's yours if you want it. It was the last one. They never have enough desserts at this thing."

"Thanks." She smiled, and just like that, she could breathe again. Soon she was laughing with Angela and making fun of Joe along with everyone else. And when Justin and Garrett left for seconds, Lexi saw her chance to talk to Angela without the worry of anyone overhearing. "I don't think I can kiss him," she said.

"Wait. Is that still bothering you?" Angela was surprised.

Lexi nodded.

"Oh my gosh. I didn't really think you would. I'm sorry I've been giving you such a hard time. I'll stop. I was just teasing you. Look, I know he likes you, but that doesn't mean anything has to happen. Let's just have fun. It's our last night with everyone here."

And before Lexi could give it any more thought, Angela jumped up and asked Lexi for her phone. "We need a group picture! Nancy can you take a picture of all of us? Guys get in!" Angela worked to organize the shot. "Lexi, move closer to Justin. Garrett, no one can see you." As everyone crowded in and Lexi moved closer to Justin, she felt the weight of his arm around her shoulders, and when the picture was over, he stayed.

The rest of the night was much like every bonfire before. It was filled with the comfort of lifelong friends, familiar laughter, and burned marshmallows. Justin's grandpa passed around the bag of songbooks Nancy and Lexi had worked on earlier in the week, and soon everyone was lost in song. The singing made it difficult to talk, but it didn't matter. Lexi soaked in the moment. She looked through the flames at the faces surrounding her. She saw Bean with Aly and Tom. Nancy sat with Justin's sister, Ellie. The Nelsons brought Yoga with them, and Buck, was trying to convince Haley to give him a chip. She saw the red heads of Jacey, Emmy, Grace, and Ryan. And Nate, Michelle, and Shannon were there too.

The heat from the bonfire and the unpredictability of the smoke's path made her eyes sting, but as long as Justin's arm was around her, she wasn't going to move. "I heard you're leaving tomorrow." Lexi leaned into Justin but kept her eyes on her feet.

"Yeah, my mom has to go back for work," he said. "We're going to head out sometime after lunch. I wish we could stay longer."

"Me too," she said.

"Hey, Lexi." Her mom tapped her shoulder. "It's time to go. Haley needs to get to bed, and Grandma's also ready."

The weight that she'd felt when the sun set pulled at her again. Lexi hugged everyone good-bye and then walked to the boat with her family. They were almost to the boat when she heard Angela. "Wait! Lexi! Your phone." Angela rushed down the dock to return Lexi's phone. "I think we got some great group pictures, and I took a few candid shots for fun. Don't forget to send them to me once you have service."

Lexi threw her arms around Angela, and Angela squeezed back.

"Thanks," Lexi whispered in her ear.

"Of course," Angela whispered in return.

Back at the cabin, Lexi couldn't sleep. She'd been so close to him. She wanted to be back in that moment. To distract herself, she reached for her phone to look at the pictures Angela took. She swiped through them, laughing at a few and deleting others, and then she saw it. It was a candid shot of her and Justin. They were on the log, and his arm was around her. She was looking at the ground, but he was looking at her, and she could see his dimple.

CHAPTER 19

LEAP

At the kitchen sink, Lexi was surrounded by the muted sounds of motors, the happy barks of dogs, friendly conversations filled with laughter, and the boom of Haley's feet across the deck as she, Aly, and Ellie ran between the cabins. The wood walls that softened the outside noise allowed her to get lost in that magnetic crack that scared the kitchen window. Alone with her thoughts, she steered clear of her daydreams and instead kept her focus on reality. The truth was she regretted how she left things at the bonfire. She'd given up sleep and instead fought with herself through the night, trying to convince herself that just being close to Justin had been enough. But her heartache beat her sensibility, and the prize was a promise that she'd make a move. With only a few hours left before Justin was supposed to leave, Lexi went to grab Justin's jacket. It'd make for a great excuse to find him.

Lexi took her time getting dressed. Her decision to do something about Justin had erased an awkward urgency that'd followed her since her arrival. The minutes with him no longer mattered, because it wasn't about how much time she got with him. She'd rather have a few moments of perfection than drawn out wishful thinking. She took care picking her clothes and pulled them over her bathing suit. She reapplied her lip gloss and checked in with the girl in the mirror while brushing her hair. She talked herself through possible scenarios and practiced her smile and laugh. The more time she took, the more her confidence grew, and she left the loft with a feeling of contentment. Whatever was about to happen would be her own doing. She was done waiting for Justin to make a move, she was done asking Angela for advice, she was done second-guessing herself; she was ready to leap.

From the front window, she saw her mom, grandma, and Nancy talking at the shoreline. She saw her aunt helping to direct her dad and uncle who carried the canoe to store under the cabin for winter. Justin's grandma and grandpa were on their deck sipping coffee with Justin's dad, and Haley continued to run circles around the cabin with Aly and Ellie close behind. But no Justin. She moved to the window that looked over the back deck but was disappointed when all she saw was Buck sunbathing.

The loud click of the cabin's front door startled her, and she turned to see her grandma carrying three empty coffee mugs. "Good morning, honey." Her grandma's jovial greeting soothed Lexi's frustration on Justin's whereabouts.

"Good morning, Grandma," Lexi said as she hurried to help her through the door.

Her grandma was pleased to have the assistance, and they both started for the kitchen. Her grandma's slow pace allowed Lexi another glance out the front window. Her heart fell—still no Justin. Where was he? she wondered.

"He's at Big Rock." Her grandma's answer to Lexi's unasked question caught her off guard.

"Who?" Lexi felt ridiculous lying to her, but the question fell out of her mouth as an instinctive safety precaution.

"Justin," her grandma said over her shoulder. "He told Nancy where he was headed, and he asked me to let you know. Maybe you should check in on him," she suggested.

"Thanks, Grandma!" Lexi kissed her cheek and threw Justin's jacket over her arm before slipping out the back door. Big Rock was the diving rock. It'd taken her until she was eight to jump off it without holding someone's hand. From the water looking up, it always looked so easy, but from the top of the rock looking down, it looked like a long way to go. She didn't remember the last time she'd jumped off it. Not wanting to be seen, she avoided the well-worn path between the cabins' front doors and instead wove her way around the backs of them, past clotheslines and half-finished piles of chopped firewood.

Big Rock wasn't far from their grouping of cabins, just not a straight shot. She needed to push through brush and cross a clearing that'd been made by an avalanche some years ago, before she'd reach the trees that kept Big Rock hidden. They were her favorite trees; she could see them from her cabin, and when their light-green leaves caught the light, they glittered as if covered in sequins.

Just beyond the trees, she could see Justin with his back to her. His shirt was off, and she held her breath taking in the lines of his tanned back. She wanted to touch him. The towel he sat on brought a smile to her face. She remembered it form when they'd used it to build a fort at his cabin. It'd been their largest fort yet, and when they'd run out of sheets, they switched to beach towels. The towel Justin sat on was the one she'd used to make her door. Lexi took a deep breath and pushed through the thin branches. "Did you jump yet?" she asked.

"No," he said, turning to face her. "I was waiting for you." He winked. The butterflies in Lexi's stomach took flight but without the familiar nausea and discomfort that usually accompanied their arrival. They circled round, their wings soft and sweet creating a slow warmth within her. The flush of her cheeks was a perfect pink. "Are you wearing your swimsuit?" he asked pushing off the ground to stand.

Lexi couldn't believe he'd been waiting for her. It'd always seemed the other way around. "I can't remember the last time I jumped," she said while pulling her T-shirt over her head. She dropped her clothes and Justin's jacket next to his towel, then stepped out of her shorts and kicked off her flip-flops. "Remember when we were little and we were too scared to jump?" She looked to him for confirmation.

"Mostly, I remember how loud you and Angela used to scream." He smiled as he walked to meet her. "What about now?" Justin reached for her hand. "You still scared?"

"Not anymore," she said as her hand closed around his. "I'm ready."

Together they counted one...two...three...and jumped. They let go as they hit the water, needing both arms to swim. Surfacing, their laughter bounced off the face of the rock and echoed back at them. The deep water was cold, but the rush Lexi felt had nothing to do with the temperature.

"That was awesome!" Justin wiped the water from his face.

"Want to go again?" she asked.

"Definitely!" he said.

Together they swam to shore. Justin pulled himself onto the bank and offered his hand to Lexi. With his help, she gained her footing in the mud at the water's edge. Out of breath with laughter and after four more jumps holding hands, they decided they'd each get one solo jump. Lexi went first and then Justin.

"I give you a seven," Lexi said.

"What! I would have tried harder if I'd known you were scoring me." He playfully splashed water at her. "I didn't give you a score."

"You didn't have to." She splashed back. "It was a ten."

"I see how it is." He ducked under water and disappeared. Lexi felt something brush her foot and let out a scream.

"Stop!"

"All right, we're even," he said. "You ready to get out? I'm getting cold."

"Yeah, I'm ready," Lexi lied with a smile. Besides, she couldn't tell him that she wanted to stay there forever.

They reached the flat top of the rock, and Justin offered his towel to Lexi. She took it without hesitation; the cold and disappointment was sinking in. Justin sat and motioned for Lexi to join him. While the day's sun had done little to warm the water, its heat had saturated the rock and warmth radiated off it. Together they sat enjoying the warmth beneath them. Everything that'd happened over the last few weeks swirled in Lexi's head. And in these last moments with him, all she wanted was to be present. She needed all her senses to lock in the details. This would be her most important memory of the summer.

"So are you excited?" he asked with his knowing smile and a nudge of his shoulder.

"Yes," she answered, and before he could ask, she met his gaze. "I'm with you," she said without blushing. "I'm always excited when I'm with you."

They kept eye contact as they leaned into one another, and before Lexi's mind could react, her heart took over. Justin reached for her face, she closed her eyes, and her lips met his. His lips were warm and soft and everything her daydreams had wanted. His kiss had a sweetness to it that added to the innocence and high expectations of a first kiss instead of taking away, and she melted into it losing her breath. And in another instant, it was over. She dropped her chin, and their foreheads rested together long enough for her to catch her breath and revel in a dream come true. She could feel his smile.

They sat in silence a few minutes longer watching the lake, before Justin stood and helped pull Lexi to her feet. "I'm glad we got a chance to hang out," he said. "We should do it more often."

Lexi held her breath; she could feel the sarcasm. "Especially with your coolness factor about to increase now that you'll be in high school."

"Oh, that's right." She laughed. "I forgot; high school makes you cool."

"Exactly." Justin laughed as he opened his arms and pulled her into him for a hug that Lexi returned. "You want to walk with me?" he asked.

"No. I think I'm going to stay," she said, letting go.

"You sure?" Justin picked up his jacket and towel before slipping into his flip-flops.

Watching Justin, goose bumps ran up Lexi's arms. She was struck by the notion that, even in this moment, when reality had far surpassed any of her fantasies, she still felt like she was dreaming. "I'm sure," she said as her hands rubbed her arms to calm the chill.

Justin saw her shiver and offered her his jacket.

"No. It's OK. I'm fine, really." Lexi halfheartedly rejected his offer and was happy Justin ignored her and wrapped the jacket around her.

"You make it look good," he said with a smile. Lexi's cheeks flushed, and she looked at her feet in an effort to hide their pink glow. She could feel her heart beating and took a deep breath to steady herself.

"Thanks," she said lifting her gaze to meet his. She was going to miss looking at him.

"OK. I guess this is it." And with a final friendly squeeze around her shoulders, he said good-bye.

"Bye, Justin," she said.

She saw a soft, one-dimpled smile cross his face before he turned and headed for the cabins. She held her arms tight around her middle, hoping to somehow contain all the emotions that flooded her as she watched him walk away and vanish into the glittering leaves.

Alone, she sat down, pulled Justin's jacket to her face, and inhaled deeply. Her stomach tightened; the smell brought her back to the kiss, and she smiled in disbelief. She shut her eyes and allowed her mind to wander through and replay every second that'd led her there. Without meaning to, she drifted into a daydream about the possibilities of next summer and stayed wrapped in the joy of anticipation, until the sound of a familiar motor pulled her out. Soon, both the hum of the motor and the boat were gone.

When she stood to leave, she walked to the rock's edge for a final look. She knew it was the distance between where she stood and the water's surface that distorted the reflection of the girl looking up at her, but Lexi couldn't help but wonder if there was more to it. But what was clear was that next summer couldn't come fast enough.

ABOUT THE AUTHOR

While growing up in San Juan Capistrano, CA author Lacie Shea Brown pined after an older boy and wrote pages and pages about him in her journals. She went on to major in journalism at Cal Poly San Luis Obispo, but an internship showed her that her real passion for words was in the emotions they evoke, not in the who, what, where and when. So she left journalism and began a career in marketing, working for Big Brothers Big Sisters and later for The Princeton Review.

After marrying her college boyfriend, Brown became the mother of two daughters. Whenever the family needed a break, the four of them would take off for the lake where Brown's husband spent his summers as a child. The teenagers Brown observed from the dock, sparked her memories of those old lovesick journals she'd faithfully kept and reminded her of the exciting emotions of first love butterflies. *Grown-Up Summer* is the result.

Made in the USA
Middletown, DE
09 March 2019